DANIEL LOCKE AND THE
THE FORTRESS OF VALHALLA

By Marty Longson

This is a work of fiction. Names, characters, places, and incidents are products of the author's imagination. Any resemblance to actual persons, living or dead is entirely coincidental.

ISBN-13: 978-1470165468

Marty Longson

Dedicated to all the people who took the time to help me reach my goals.

Daniel Locke and the Towers:
Book 1 – The Tower of Eden
Book 2 – The Fortress of Valhalla
Book 3 – The Tombs of Hades
Book 4 – The Armies of Atlantis
Book 5 – The Fate of Olympus
Book 6 – The End of Days / Heaven's Trail

For more information about this series of novels go to, http://www.martylongson.com

The Fortress of Valhalla

Prologue - Hawaii

The skies were clear and cloudless as a pair of F-18 jets climbed into the afternoon sky. The two U.S. Navy planes were part of the long-range recon group, dedicated to protecting the Navy carrier fleet in the waters just south of the Hawaiian Islands. The sleek grey fighters passed through the clouds and levelled off as they began their scheduled patrol.

Captain Sloan "Angel" West was flying wingman in the two-seated jet, her co-pilot Billy "Cools" Samson sat behind her cracking the occasional joke. They trailed the lead F-18 Hornet flown by Captain Gord "Sword" Milan and Tim "Sway bar" Connor.

Sloan's movements were smooth and precise as the F-18 Hornets banked and began to circle the fleet below. News had come in just that morning that part of the North Korean fleet had been spotted mobilizing and heading in their general direction. Sloan had also heard strange rumours of a massive U.F.O. preceding the Korean fleet, although no one had any idea exactly what the object was, other pilots had heard whispers that the North Koreans might have had replicated the technology behind the Aurora California.

The Aurora California was a shimmering curtain of light that had mysteriously sprung up around a small northern Californian valley several months ago. The aurora looked like the Northern Lights and had been linked to strange artifacts with seemingly magical properties. Events surrounding military actions against the area inside the Aurora California, now known as Eden, had been covered up but in the fallout, several high-ranking officers were dismissed from duty. One of the highest officers dismissed was her old C.O., Colonel Charles Tapper.

Sloan's thoughts were interrupted by the radio in her helmet. It squawked as the control tower relayed their orders.

"Bugs 1 and 2, we have unidentified bogies approaching 100 mile zone. Sat-cam reports multiple contacts. Situation is hostile, we have confirmed several civilian vessels down in the area. Proceed to sector Alpha-2 for long-range recon. We need eyes on A.S.A.P. Reports are indicating a massive U.F.O., use full spectrum kit analysis once you have a visual."

"Roger, Con," Gord said, voice tight in anticipation. "Bugs 1 and 2 Oscar Mike."

"You ready Angel?" Gord asked over the com line.

"I got your back Sword," Sloan replied as she readied the plane for combat.

Sloan pulled back the glove on her left hand and kissed a pair of red hearts tattooed into her skin.

"Luck," she prayed aloud.

"Stay frosty, afterburners in 3, 2, 1," Gord counted down.

The jet fighters lit their afterburners and launched into supersonic flight, leaving a pair of matching clouds in their wake. In a matter of minutes, a small dot appeared on the horizon. The dark shape grew larger in the distance as they began to see flashes and explosions in the air ahead of them. It took a moment to comprehend the enormity of what Sloan was seeing. There was a large rocky island floating below them at around 10,000 feet. The air around the floating island danced with shimmering lights and the occasional explosion. Swarming around the area like a nest of angry ants was the entire North Korean Navy and Air Force. Down on the water, several ships were billowing thick black smoke in the wake of the naval fleet.

"Control, this is Bug 1. We have visual confirmation, North Korean forces are engaged with a... uhh... unknown force." Gord's normally rock steady voice faltered as the immense size of the floating island filled the horizon. "Con, you're not gonna believe this, U.F.O. is a floating rock," Gord said obviously not believing his eyes. "I estimate the U.F.O. is 10 miles wide and putting the hurt on the Koreans."

"Roger visual Bug 1," Con said, not reacting to the news at all. "Maintain visual, Con out."

"Jesus, Sword we got a friendly down there." Sway bar said excitedly. "Friend or Foe tags read USS Independence. It is Colonel Tapper's old Destroyer, radar puts it stationed right under the rock. Looks like she's hit, Independence is listing hard to port."

Warning sirens sounded inside the F-18's cockpit as their combat systems picked up multiple threats, all of them closing fast.

"Four bogies are breaking off from the main force and are tracking our way." Cools said. "Looks like a set of Migs."

"Roger that, keep an eye on them Billy. Climbing to max ceiling." Sloan grimaced as she pulled back on the flight stick and started to feel the g's push her back into her seat.

Control tower's voice crackled over the radio again. "Bugs 1 and 2, you have two dark spots in transit, stand firm, spots arriving in... t-minus 50 seconds."

The "dark spots" were the Navy's fighting unmanned vehicles, or U.A.V.'s. Each drone was equipped with the latest stealth technology and a state of the art scramjet engine. The scramjet engine allowed the unmanned drone to exceed Mach 10 in a matter of moments. The drones had little or no armaments though, they were strictly ultra-fast mobile cameras. It would be up to the two F-18's to provide air support to the drones, or at least a very big distraction.

Gord continued to lead the jets into a steep climb and away from the fight, maintaining a respectable distance from the North Korean fleet, but close enough to see what was going on. Together the two fighter jets pulled away from the floating rock and began to circle around to the south.

"Bug 1," con called out. "Maintain current heading and speed until further notice. Bug 2 confirm load out... one Harpoon Anti-ship missile."

"Bug 2 confirms load out, Harpoon Anti-ship missile on board."

"Bug 2, check your H.U.D for updated target information. Target is hostile, you are a go for immediate bombing run, warm the Harpoon up."

"Roger con, good target. Warming Harpoon, commencing bombing run. Bug 2 out."

"Good hunting Angel," Gord called out as he flashed a V hand sign. "Looks like I get the short straw again. I will swing around and flank those Migs, it should give you some breathing room at least."

As luck would have it, Sword's F-18 was equipped with only air-to-air missiles while her jet was setup for surface attacks or bombing runs. She didn't envy her friend though, Gord was going to have a hell of a time dealing with all those Migs. She gave him the thumbs up and a quick nod.

"Okay Cools, let's get back to the fight." Sloan said as she banked the F-18 back towards the Korean fleet. "Arm the Harpoon. We are going to light it up. Target the closest Korean ship and get me good lock."

"Roger that... setting course... Migs are still tracking."

"Forget the Migs, just set the lock Billy."

"...Setting lock... target confirmed." Billy sounded nervous, "Sloan, the Migs will be on us before we can get our shot off. I can't see Sword. All the Migs are on our ass."

"I know," Sloan said quietly. "Have a little faith."

Sloan kicked in the afterburners and set her course, pushing the plane's nose down towards the water. The F-18 groaned as the stressed plane issued its disapproval.

Sloan heard her co-pilot curse her as he lost the target lock. Billy would have to reacquire the lock again before they could drop the Harpoon.

"Migs are trailing us Sloan. They are going to have us before we..."

"Faith." Sloan urged.

Billy resumed grumbling, trying to keep an eye on the Migs and trying to reacquire his missile lock.

Two black streaks screamed by her port side like her F-18 was standing still and Billy cursed again. Sloan banked the jet hard to follow the dark unmanned drones and provide what little air support she could.

"More Migs are scrambling Sloan." Billy continued to curse but had resumed his cool frosty edged voice. "They are going after the drones."

Sloan hit her air brakes and decelerated, putting her F-18 back in line with the Korean naval fleet. "Get me a tone!"

Her abrupt actions had caught everyone but her co-pilot off guard.

"Reacquiring lock in 3,2,- beeeeeep," Billy said in a cold voice.

"Good tone... firing."

"Break right!" Billy screamed at her as the Harpoon missile dropped away from the belly of her plane.

With no hesitation, Sloan flung the flight stick hard right and banked away. As the plane turned, an explosion rocked them as a missile tore through their left wing. The F-18 pitched over hard and Sloan was able to track the missile's smoky flight back to its source. A dark panelled warship sat motionless in the ocean below them, almost invisible to the naked eye.

"Stealth boat." Sloan grunted as she fought against the g-forces. "Billy get us out of here, pop the lid... Billy?"

Sloan looked back to a slumped body in the seat behind her. The canopy beside Billy's head was spidered with cracks and her friend was utterly still in his harness. Fire was working its way up the fuselage as Sloan reached for the ejection handles. Just before she released, a dark shape came crashing through the canopy and slammed into her. Instantly her world went dark.

Chapter 1 – Eden - Believe It or Not.

The great white tree stood large and imposing over the rocky coast of Eden. The chilled October air whistled through its large greenish brown leaves and around its thick trunk as a pair of teenagers sat watching the seagulls soar over the nearby beach. Indy and Joslyn sat among the tree's enormous exposed roots, cuddled in a thick woollen blanket. Although Indy was unable to feel the winds biting cold, he could still feel Joslyn's body shaking slightly in the cool ocean air. He looked away from the gulls to stare into her eyes. Brushing away a few frost scarred strands of hair, he gingerly ran a finger down her frosted cheek. His finger continued down her neck to the leather cord holding a little leather bag he had given her for safekeeping. Even with one eye a milky blue, she looked like an angel.

"I wish we could stay here all day," Indy said to her as he leaned in to kiss her lips.

Joslyn wrapped both arms around him in silent agreement as they kissed softly. Sitting under the tree had become a favourite pastime for them. When he was there everything in the world seemed to disappear, it was a peace like no other. Indy could feel his mother looking down on him and watching over him in his heart. His mom, Jolie Locke had sacrificed herself to bring the giant white tree into existence in the hope that one day, the tree would save the world. The white staff that had cured her cancer and healed countless others had been the seed that formed the massive tree overnight. Indy missed his mom more than he could ever say and the time he spent sitting there filled a void in his heart left by her passing.

Adam, Eden's mystical curator, had told Indy that his mother was still alive inside the tree but there was no telling if she would ever return. The tree was a source of tranquility now and he treasured ever moment he could spend there. Everyone in the castle appeared to feel the same way. At any given time there were people wandering around the tree. Some prayed at the base of its massive trunk while others seemed to linger in its shade. People naturally gravitated to the tree and returned day after day. They found strength in the large branches and comfort in the way the wind sang through its leaves.

Indy and Joslyn sat with their backs against the tree as a group of people made their way down a well-worn dirt path from the castle to the base of the tree. Indy nodded his head at the woman leading the group, who wore a brown robe like the others behind her but carried a long wooden walking stick.

"Morning Beatrice," Indy said with a bright smile.

"Good morning Guardian." The old woman gave Indy a polite wave of her hand and ushered her flock under the shadow of the tree.

The group of people had taken to calling themselves "True Believers". Indy spotted several faces he knew within the deep cowls of the brown robes. He could see the rock star, the ex-soldier and a host of others grouped up behind Beatrice and kneeling in the shadow of the great tree. All of the True Believers were people that his mother had saved with the healing touch of the white staff. The Believers would wander down to the tree every morning to spend a few minutes under its healing branches before heading back to their cabins on the far side of the castle. All they wanted was to be left alone, they desired only peace and tranquility. They had no cares for the outside world, insisting that Eden itself would provide all the sustenance they needed to exist.

"They look so happy, so peaceful." Joslyn remarked. "I am a bit jealous of them some days."

"Oh, you would fit in with them so well," Indy said, his voice layered with sarcasm. "Well, that is if you want to renounce all your worldly possessions. That includes webcams and big screen TV's you know."

Joslyn's face tightened at the miserable thought of losing some of her favourite things.

Indy continued the torment, "No buttered popcorn, no chick flicks... no hair driers, no-

"Stop, stop, I get it, there is no way I can give up my movies." Her expression eased a bit as she leaned in for another kiss.

Joslyn stopped just short of the kiss and pulled back to look Indy in the eyes.

"I know you can't feel my kisses, because of the shield, but do you-

"I love it when you kiss me Joslyn, it makes me feel like I am normal. I really miss that feeling."

Indy leaned into her long blonde hair and breathed in deeply. The sweet smell of strawberries filled his nose.

"At least I haven't lost my sense of smell," he said with a smile.

Joslyn was referring to the bulletproof effect that his living tattoo granted him. The moment he passed through the aurora surrounding this valley, his body had absorbed one of the crystal artifacts he had been carrying. That crystal dragon became the dragon tattoo and in turn, had made him unbreakable. The swirling black dragon tattoo chose that moment to appear, sliding out from under his sleeve and wrapping itself around his forearm. Joslyn noticed it and slowly reached out to touch it.

"It's warm there," she said and gave Indy's tattoo a soft kiss.

The warmth of the tattoo was the only real sensation he felt now, besides a slight pressure of any physical contact. When Joslyn kissed it, his whole body trembled in a brief moment of pleasure. The sensation only lasted the briefest of moments but was something he would cherish for hours.

The dragon tattoo may have given him a bulletproof shield but without a sense of touch, Indy had begun feeling... estranged, apart from everyone else. He regretted the loss of those feelings very much right at that moment.

"Do you ever regret bringing me up to the castle?" Indy asked.

Joslyn looked at him with a hard calculating gaze before answering.

"No, I miss my family more than anything right now but when I saw you pull up to the diner on that Ducati... well, put it this way, all I ever wished for was given to me. A hot boyfriend, a castle romance and an adventure straight out of a fairy tale. I know everything will work out, sometimes you just have to have a little faith."

Joslyn smiled at Indy and her crystalized skin sparkled in the sun. She was so beautiful, the frost scar crystals and milky blue eye gave her a sweet surreal look. Indy had fallen hard for this girl and he knew she could see it in his eyes.

"That reminds me," Joslyn said with a gleam in her one good eye. "Someone owes me a date night, and I have just the right movie in mind. How does sweet hom-

Something loud popped in the branches overhead, interrupting her words. They both looked up when they heard Jon's delighted scream.

"Got it!" He yelled.

They turned their heads up to watch their lanky blonde friend drifting slowly down from the branches high above, clinging to a large swollen leaf and seedpod. The Believers kneeling at the base of the tree refused to even lift their heads from their prayers as Jon floated by.

Indy's best friend Jon had been playing with the odd leaves all morning. The white tree's leaves were extraordinary in the fact that they didn't fall like other leaves, they rose. Before they released from their branch the thick long leaves expanded like a balloon with a popping noise. The leaves reminded Indy of a parasail as they drifted on the air currents. When the bloated leaves didn't have a teenager hanging from them, each leaf would float out over the sea, destined to drop its seeds on a far distant land.

"Wooooo, go Jon!" Joslyn yelled in encouragement and nudged Indy. "It looks like he's got a good wind this time."

Indy nodded his head in agreement. "Let's grab the Jeep and meet him on the beach, looks like he is gonna get wet."

No sooner did Indy say the words than Jon's laughter faded. Jon's leaf had caught a stiff breeze and was rising in the air like a gull on a thermal draft. Luckily, Jon already had an escape plan in place. Releasing one hand, he let the air spill from the leaf. As a result, the leaf started to spiral down to the water below. The good news was that once down in the water, the balloon leaf made an excellent raft.

Indy stood and held out his hand to Joslyn. "You coming?"

Joslyn accepted his hand but shook her head no in response. "My dad has me pencilled in for a web cam chat. I have to head in now anyway."

"Okay," Indy said with his lopsided grin. "Tell the sheriff I said hi."

Joslyn shook her head again. "No way, he still hasn't forgiven you for the whole tower incident. I'm not even allowed to mention your name anymore. He would have a fit if he ever found out about us."

Indy shrugged, he knew the sheriff blamed him for the problems facing his daughter. "I don't know what else I can do," Indy said.

Joslyn hugged him close and said, "Give him time Indy, he'll come around. After all, you saved my life once or twice. But I really have to run, I am going to be late and Jon looks like he is going to need a towel." Joslyn released Indy and turned to walk back to the castle. "Meet ya later for lunch, okay?

"Sure, I just have to stop by Hank's new place. Dad wanted me to check on his progress." Indy said as Joslyn continued off toward the castle. "See ya then." He called.

The Fortress of Valhalla

Chapter 2 – Eden - Wall

Jon was sitting in the sand watching his leaf rise into the air as Indy pulled up in his Jeep. The leaf rose slowly over the water before catching the breeze again and drifting out to sea.

"You have got to try that Indy," Jon said with a beaming smile. "At least once before all the leaves are gone."

Indy nodded his head but had no real desire to venture up into the great white tree's branches.

"Hey, have you seen my backpack?" Jon asked as he poked his head inside the Jeep.

Indy shook his head no, but helped Jon look.

"I thought I left it in here." Jon looked all around the inside of the Jeep but came up empty handed. "Damn, I had my iPad in it too." Jon moaned as he gave up his search.

"I'll keep an eye out for it," Indy said. "Joslyn is heading back to the castle, but I have to go see Hank, you feel like sticking around for a bit?" Indy asked as he waved his keys around.

An evil grin spread across Jon's face as he replied, "Only if I can drive."

Indy handed over his keys in mock terror and Jon grabbed them from Indy's shaking hand.

"You aren't very funny, Junior." Jon said as he jumped into the driver's seat.

Indy was only called Junior by his family and a select few people that knew his father and he cringed every time he heard the name mentioned. To his friends he was just Indy, to everyone else he was Daniel.

"Ouch Jon, low blow." Indy said with a smile as he strapped himself into the Jeep's four-point harness.

Jon stared at Indy and said, "Really? The harness too? You are indestructible, aren't you?"

Indy's smile only grew as he continued to tighten the straps and brace himself for the drive. With a sputter of indignation, Jon started the Jeep and tore across the sand.

Jon decided to take the scenic route to Hank's in order to get more driving time behind the wheel of the Jeep. They drove up the ridge and followed the coast around until it met up with the shimmering lights of the Aurora California. The aurora was ever present and surrounded the little country his dad had named Eden. Since the aurora first appeared, things had changed within Eden's border. Animals throughout the whole valley were thriving. None of the birds or other animals suffered any ill effects from passing in to or out of the aurora but for humans, it was another matter. Upon leaving the aurora's shimmering lights a person would crystallize into a statue, or at the very least suffer frost scaring like Joslyn.

Scientists his father had hired, suggested that the crystallization process was linked to the ability to use artifacts, quite possibly DNA related. They further hypothesized that this was to prevent accidental activations of the artifacts themselves. So no creature could inadvertently cause the situation currently surrounding the valley.

Jon swerved the Jeep to avoid a large rabbit that had bolted out of the woods as the Jeep passed. The Jeep clipped several small trees before bouncing back onto the wide dirt track that they were following. Indy just shook his head at Jon and watched as the rabbit took two large bounds before disappearing into the thick briar on the other side of the path.

Over the last two months, a thick briar wall had sprung up along the base of the aurora. Since it appeared, it had grown like a weed and now was a thick mass of thorny vines over twenty feet high.

The wall had eventually completely cut off land access to Appleton and left Eden with only the beach area open for coming and going. Earlier efforts to cut through the thick thorns were abandoned when the wall simply regrew the damaged areas over night.

The Jeep zipped around the edge of the aurora and followed the well-worn trail all the way back to the Appleton road. At the Appleton road intersection a large defunct transport helicopter had been pulled from the road and was now in the process of being consumed by the vegetation. Two white tombstones marked the end of the trail and Jon stopped the Jeep to pause and pay respect. There were two names carved into the painted white wood, Sean O'dede and Lawrence Punch. Those two men had been part of a security detail operating a barricade guarding the way in to and out of the valley. Both had been turned to crystal statues when they had been forcibly removed from the aurora by the U.S. military.

"Do you think they are still there?" Jon asked. "I mean inside the statues."

Indy nodded his head. "I think so, I just wish we knew how to bring them back into Eden without killing them. Doc said that after examining Joslyn's frost scar effects, he is 100 percent sure that just dragging them back into the aurora would result in total organ failure."

Jon stared blankly at the briar thorn wall. "What a crappy way to go."

Just as Jon was about to pull back onto the road, a Razor side by side A.T.V. came roaring up. The little kart slid to a stop in front of the Jeep, blocking it from the road.

Inside the kart was Jon's dad, Barney Lucas and Indy's least favourite teenager, Warren Hocking. They were both wearing the dark blue security team outfits with silver E.D.T. labels on the shoulders.

"Jon, Indy, what the hell are you two up to out here? Barney asked. "The council has ordered everyone to stay away from the wall. We just finished setting up motion sensors around the entire perimeter. Sasser is going to be pissed that he has to reset each one now."

Warren sat in the passenger seat shooting them an evil smirk that only broadened when they heard Sasser's voice.

Sasser's angry voiced echoed over the kart's radio, "LUCAS! What moron is out there tripping the sensors? When you find him-

"We have him already, it was my son Jon and Daniel Jr."

Sasser grumbled his reply, "Just make sure it doesn't happen again. Sasser out."

The look on Warren's face showed nothing but contempt as his smirk faded away.

"Right then, you kids heard the man, off you go now. Remember to stay away from the wall." Barney nodded to his son as he restarted the Razor.

Spinning the kart around, Barney clipped several bushes and almost overturned the A.T.V. Warren was almost thrown from the kart and had his dark glare wiped away by a moment of pure panic. The Razor's wheels squealed as the spinning tires met the paved road and the kart rocketed away.

"Now I see where you get your driving skills." Indy teased as he retightened his harness.

"Dude," Jon complained. "That's not fair. Besides, I am a better pilot then you."

"Just because I don't like heights," Indy shot back defensively. "You are just lucky the sleds have internal avoidance and you don't need to stay on any roads."

"At least I still have mine." Jon retorted and instantly regretted it. "Man, I didn't mean that, I know you could have died from that crash."

Indy could very well have died in that crash. His dragon tattoo had just barely managed to protect him as its power faded moments after he left the aurora and crashed into a cliffside.

"Forget about it Jon," Indy said and punched Jon in the leg. "Who could have known the A.G.P. wouldn't avoid the aurora, it avoids everything else after all."

"Just a bad design flaw I guess." Jon agreed as he rubbed his leg and gave Indy a small scowl.

Jon started the Jeep back up and cruised down the paved road heading away from the old barricade and towards the orchard.

As they drove, they passed through an area of cleared timber and paved lots.

"What ever happened to your dad's plan to build this place up into a town?" Jon asked.

"It fell through I guess. He was expecting a lot more people to come into Eden but so far, it has just been the odd handful of people here and there. The castle itself isn't even up to capacity, let alone the other outer buildings. I think a lot of people are scared. Between the threat of Valhalla coming, being trapped in here once you enter and all the other mystical mumbo jumbo, I can't really blame them. Once the thorn wall sprouted up, it pretty much spelled the end of that plan."

Jon drove in silence as he considered the road ahead. "You know, I kind of like it here. I mean, the threat of becoming a statue notwithstanding, I really like it here. I don't understand half of the artifacts or the aurora, but it is all pretty sweet. Now if Doc would only let us be part of the Eden Defense Team, I would be a happy camper."

The E.D.T. had been formed to help protect the Eden using the artifacts Doc had secured. Indy had watched the E.D.T. practising for the past month, working on drills and formations and training in hand to hand combat. The team had also been allowed full access to a multitude of cool artifacts. Doc had selected a few of the kids in the castle to help fill the ranks left vacant by several missing security team members. Of course, those kids were Warren, Amber and Thomas. The only good news was that with their new positions and training, it had kept them away from Indy and his friends for the most part. Indy only had to endure the occasional stare lately.

Ahead of the Jeep, a large farmhouse appeared beside the entrance to the orchard. The house before them was almost an exact replica of Hank's old farmhouse but now had been moved to the outer edge of the orchard. Behind the two-story house, a large red barn rose up to dominate the view.

"Looks like Hank has been busy." Jon said admiring the barn. "That barn is big enough to house a 747."

Indy agreed, "Ya, dad said that old Hank wanted to expand his orchard business and market the cider as an Eden Reserve. I guess the two of them went into business together with dad putting up the cash and Hank running the farm."

"I love that cider." Jon said as a bit of drool formed at the corner of his mouth.

"Let's go see if Hank has any chilled and waiting." Indy agreed with a quick smile and a nod.

The Jeep turned down the paved driveway and stopped behind Hank's battered old pickup truck. The old man was sitting on his front porch and waved as the two boys made their way up the stairs.

"Hey Hank," Jon said as he looked around the yard. "Still no sign of Snoop?"

Hank simply shook his head before welcoming the boys. "Glad you kids could stop by. I've been meaning to head up to the castle but I haven't found the time. Your dad keeps me pretty busy these days." Hank grinned at them and stood up from his chair. "Snoops is still missing, I haven't see any sign of him for months. Poor dog musta been scared witless by James and that monster Zeus."

Hank's face tightened as he spoke the two names that had caused him so much heartache. Hank had lost everything he had after the tower of Eden rose and later fell, taking his home and store with it. The only thing marking the spot where his house once stood was a small lake.

"Why don't you kids sit with me for a bit, I could use the company. Wait here a sec and I will go grab us a couple drinks." Hank wandered into his house with his shoulders visibly sagging.

"Poor guy, I don't know what he misses more, his old house or his dog." Jon said in sympathy.

"It's gotta be hard on him, out here all alone but Hank insists on doing it all his way. I guess he set up all the machinery himself and made the whole process totally automated," Indy said as they waited for final proof of the new setup.

They didn't have long to wait. Hank came back out of the house with a tray of glasses and a tall pitcher of dark brown liquid. He poured them all a glass before settling back down into his rocking chair.

The kids both downed the glass of cider and took a moment to enjoy the sweet liquid goodness they expected from Hank's famous cider.

"Hank, you are a genius," Indy said as he raised his empty glass in salute.

Jon mimicked the salute and finished the rest of his glass. He was just about to lower it back to the tray when he froze. Something under Hank's plaid shirt was moving. It looked like an alien ready to explode out of his chest.

Hank grimaced, obviously annoyed. "Well the cat's out of the bag now I guess," he said as he reached under his shirt to pull out a black and white panda man. "The little bugger won't leave me alone. Mr. Locke asked me to keep an eye on him for a little while." Hank's big hand held the little bear close to his chest as the panda wrapped its chunky arms around Hank's thumb. "I named him Chi."

The panda's appearance shocked Indy, and disturbed him at the same time. His father had been really attached to the little panda man and seeing it with Hank was a bit difficult. The little panda monk was known to be overly protective of his father. Indy tried to hide his discomfort and asked, "Chi, isn't that the Chinese word for spirit?"

Hank nodded. "Chi here is one big bundle of spirit. I don't think he even sleeps. But enough about my little friend, let's get down to business, you are probably here to get a report for your dad." Hank reached over to his side table and grabbed a large envelope. "You can tell your dad everything is on schedule, I can begin full production any day now."

"Ok, I will let him know." Indy said as he eyed Chi with a small smile.

"Oh, and don't forget to say hi to Little Cloud for me." Hank said rising from his chair and grabbing the boys into a large bear hug.

The little panda man was just barely able to avoid being squashed in the embrace and climbed up to perch on Hank's shoulder. They said their farewells and made their way back to the Jeep. As they were leaving both Hank and Chi were waving goodbye.

Chapter 3 – Eden - Rage Against

The entertainment room Jon, Joslyn and Indy had used as their main hangout had undergone a recent transformation. Sasser, the castle's tech guru and communications specialist, had come in to do a little telecommunications magic and the result was a soundproof webcam booth with pull down shades for privacy. The good news was that they only had to remove a foosball table to make enough room for the large custom-made booth.

Joslyn had already spent untold hours in the booth, talking with her friends and family from Appleton. It was her only way to spend time with her mom and dad, so she took every advantage of the booth anytime she could.

Today was no different as Indy wandered into the entertainment room. The webcam booth blinds were closed but the door was slightly ajar and he could hear Joslyn's giggles drifting out of the open door.

"Vince, stop it," He heard Joslyn say in a hushed voice. "Someone will hear you."

A voice Indy didn't recognize responded, "I don' care who hears me, I want the world to know!" The voice that must have been Vince was getting louder as Joslyn continued to giggle.

"Shhh," she urged.

Vince's voice was young and definitely male. "I love-

"Don't you dare say it right now Vincent Alexander! If you tell me over this damn webcam I will kick your ass." Joslyn scolded.

Indy's blood started to boil and his ears started to pound in time with his heart. Before he could step forward to confront Joslyn, a white form slipped out from inside the booth and regarded him with dark red eyes. It was Joslyn's white wolf, Boo.

The wolf eyed him, sensing his anger, and freezing him in place with its eyes. Indy realized his anger was clouding his judgment and gave the wolf a long hard look before storming from the room.

Indy's emotions carried him down the hall in seconds and had him practically running down the back stairs when he heard a moaning coming from the stairwell below. He recognized Allen's moan of pain and the voices taunting him. It was Warren and his little posse.

As Indy came further down the stairs he paused, stunned by the scene before him. At the foot of the stairs, Allen was pinned to the floor

by Warren and Thomas. Amber stood above Allen holding a small dagger that was dripping a waxy yellow liquid onto Allen's chest. Each drop of liquid steamed as it hit Allen and was quickly building up an orange crystalline mass as it dried.

It was all just too much for Indy to handle. He was already angry over Joslyn's apparent betrayal and now this senseless act of bullying by Warren and his gang. Indy couldn't even think straight, he just reacted.

Indy's vision went red as he leapt down the remaining flight of stairs. He crashed hard into Thomas, who tumbled away, taking Amber with him. The pair landed heavily in the corner. Indy kicked a startled Warren in the face before the kid had a chance to pull any kind weird artifact on him. Warren flew backwards and crashed against the closed stairwell door causing it to fly open into a startled Sam Brown. Sam must have been just reaching for the door when Warren came crashing through it.

Sam reacted with sloth-like reflexes and crashed underneath the still tumbling Warren.

An evil smile crossed Indy's face briefly as he watched Warren go sprawling away.

"It's okay Allen, everything is okay now. Sam's here too, we are going to get you to the nurse, okay?" Indy was reaching down to help Allen when he heard the call for help go out.

"Code Red. Code Red" Sam Brown was calling into his walkie-talkie. "Stairwell D, first floor, Junior is attacking E.D.T. members."

"What are you talking about Sam?" Indy yelled. "Warren..."

Sam flinched away at the menace in Indy's voice and Indy had to take several deep breaths in order to calm down enough to talk reasonably. "Look Sam, Allen is hurt, Warren and Thomas-

Warren interrupted him, "He kicked me in the face and knocked Thomas into..."

For the first time they noticed the moans coming from the dark corner Amber and Thomas had crashed into. The corner was a mass of confusion as Indy's eyes tried to sort it all out. Amber and Thomas were lying face down in a spreading pool of yellow liquid. The dagger was still clutched in Amber's hand but had been pinned to the floor by one of Thomas's thick forearms. It looked as if the dagger's blade had been cracked open and the waxy fluid was now pouring out uncontrollably.

The waxy liquid was spilling from the blade and coursing over their hands. Indy watched in horror as the yellow liquid started to harden into an orange crystal puddle.

Indy reacted first, running over to them and pulling them out of the spreading liquid. Some of the crystal formation still clung to their hands and arms but at least they weren't stuck to the ground. The yellow wax continued to drip from the dagger as Thomas and Amber stood shakily, connected at the hands.

Pounding feet and raised voices warned Indy seconds before three men swarmed into the stairwell. Each man wore thick artifact armour and wielded a purple energy whip. Without hesitating, they lashed out at Indy and wrapped him in long crackling ropes. Indy was tied up and a bag placed over his head before he could even utter a curse.

The bag covering Indy's head blocked out all light and sound. To Indy, it was a startling deprivation of his senses and as hard as he tried to fight it, he started to fall asleep. Something about the bag sapped his energy, his limbs felt weak and he was having a hard time remaining upright. The last thought Indy had before dozing off was uttered in an incoherent mumble, "Hahaha, a sleeping bag."

Indy awoke suddenly when the black artifact bag was ripped from his head. He found the very angry and bruised face of Warren Hocking staring down at him. They were in the holding cells deep within the Hydro plant. The special rooms had originally been converted to detain soldiers that were captured by the castle's security forces. The soldiers had long since escaped from Eden with the help of a pair of traitors. James and Zeus had turned their backs on the Locke family in an effort to wrest control of Eden from Indy's father. Along with helping the soldiers escape, James had shot his father in the leg.

Warren was staring at Indy with utter hatred burning through his eyes. "You rich little snob, you broke my nose."

Warren's face was a mass of yellowish bruises, but it was obviously healing pretty well. That was one of the major benefits of living within Eden's aurora, everyone healed at an incredible rate. No one suffered any of the common ailments like colds or even the major ones like cancer.

Indy braced himself for the punch he could see coming a mile away. He could have dodged it easily but thanks to the dragon tattoo, he really didn't need to. Warren's punch rocked Indy's head back. The strength of the punch shocked

Indy a bit, without the protection of his dragon tattoo, that punch might have knocked him out cold.

Warren didn't even flinch from the pain of his hand hitting the shield. Instead, he turned from Indy and began to pace the small room back and forth.

"I don't care how long it takes or what I have to do, I am going to make you pay for this. For what you did to Thomas and Amber... and my nose." Warren paused in his pacing. "Oh, you don't know do you." A hard look came over Warren's face. "You don't even know what you did yet."

Warren bent down to get into Indy's face. "That little stunt you pulled in the stairwell is going to cost them their hands. Whatever you did to them caused the artifact dagger to malfunction and crystalized their hands together. My dad thinks that the only way to separate them will be amputation."

Warren sneered at Indy and stepped away. He retrieved the artifact hood and held it out in front of Indy's face.

"This is too good for you," he said shaking the bag open. "But if I have my way... you will never see anything but the inside of this bag again."

Warren stuffed the bag roughly over Indy's head and the world went dark again.

Chapter 4 – Eden - The Council Chambers

Time stopped moving for Indy the second the hood slipped over his head. Indy's dulled connection to the outside world only made being inside the hood that much more of a prison. For the moment Indy's only companion were his own dreamy thoughts. Images flashed through his mind as he relived the last few hours. The rage that had filled him seemed so distant now, as he relived the fight in the stairwell. He recalled Warren's shocked face and smiled to himself.

Another thought echoed deep in his mind. "A true enemy that one is. You would be wise to keep a closer eye on him."

The thought seem to reverberate in his head before fading away.

When the hood finally came off again, Indy found himself sitting in the council's boardroom back in the castle. A long table stretched out before him, surrounded by ten angry councillors from ten different countries. His father had gathered the council together to garner support and protection from each of their perspective countries. Their support came at a steep price, which was the full disclosure and sharing of any and all artifacts found within Eden's boundaries. A few artifacts had already been shipped out of Eden but for the most part, the bulk of the artifacts remained within the shimmering curtain that provided the energy used to activate their magical powers. Each councillor made routine inspections of the lead artifact scientist, Dr. Henrik Hocking, or just Doc, as he was more apt to be called.

Therein was the real problem, a power struggle that floated in the background of any and all discussions held by the council. Although his father Daniel Locke sr. had the final say on all matters in front of the council, Doc had most of the council in his pocket. They stayed in his pocket if they wanted to continuously receive technical updates on artifact developments or access to the items themselves. A word from Doc and a councillor could become stubborn and unforthcoming when it was required to deal with their home countries. Quite often, any matter before the council became bogged down for days before a resolution could be found.

Indy knew the odds were stacked against him as he looked around the room, trying to gauge the room's attitude. Most of the councillors cast hard, calculating looks his way but several looked past him to a person just out of Indy's vision.

A slight bit of pressure on his shoulder caused Indy to look back to see his father standing behind him. Daniel Locke sr. stood beside Indy patting his son's shoulder. Their green eyes met for an instant and an anxious expression briefly crossed his father's face. That single look conveyed a thousand words, none of them good.

His father walked around the table, took off his tailored Armani suit jacket and sat down at his spot at the head of the table. An aide stepped forward to take the coat and placed a manila envelope in his hand before stepping back out of the room.

Indy remained silent as his father opened the envelope and read the letter inside. Annoyance flickered over his face as he read. That expression quickly grew to a tightening of his eyes and mouth before the pages were flung to the table.

"Gentlemen," Daniel said. "As you have seen from the security footage, there are considerable gaps in Mr. Hocking's testimony and I need to consider all aspects of this case before handing out a verdict for council approval. As I see it, the Guardian acted wilfully and with wanton disregard for the safety of others. In this case, it does not matter the reasons why he acted as he did. We must hold this individual to a higher standard than others because of his required duties and subsequent abilities."

Several of the men around the table nodded their heads in agreement but most of the councillors remained silent and watchful.

Daniel Sr. looked down the table and straight into Indy's eyes.

"I am very disappointed in you. This community looks up to you and requires your actions to be beyond reproach. Our Guardian cannot risk endangering anyone's life, no matter his personal feelings."

"Although," his father paused as he looked around the room at the councillors. "We understand that there are mitigating circumstances that may have aggravated the situation. Dr. Hocking has made several suggestions as to dealing with you as a punishment. He would be here now to give evidence but two young people injured today required immediate surgery to try and separate them from each other and an orange crystal substance."

Daniel Locke sr. picked up several of the pages on the table before him. He studied them a moment longer and then released a long sigh.

"Dr. Hocking has asked that you be imprisoned for a period of one year or until such time we have need of your unique abilities."

There were several mumbled agreements at Doc's suggestion but no one at the table seemed to be in full support of imprisonment.

Daniel Locke sr. stood from his chair and began to pace the room. He stopped pacing and walked over to stand in front of Indy.

"I have come to my decision." Daniel looked around at the councillors before continuing, "We are at a critical juncture in our community. With the real threat of an unknown and potentially deadly enemy, the people of this valley need encouragement. Public moral is just as important to us as a strong defensive team. There is much work to be done in order to prepare for a possible confrontation, and although the E.D.T. is doing an excellent job of preparing us, we need more. We need the support of this community to get that work done. That is why my recommendation is to put our best foot forward."

His father looked down at him and gave Indy a small smile. "No longer will you wander these grounds aimlessly. I want you front and center in the work effort. I want to see you work your ass off for the better of this valley. To be honest, you should have been placed in the public eye much sooner, Adam named you Guardian of the Tower of Eden, and now I name you Guardian of this castle. As such you will be required to serve the people of this valley for as long as the aurora surrounds us."

The councillors around the table applauded his father's decision. Indy noted several frowns cast his way but for the most part his father's recommendation was approved unanimously.

Daniel Locke sr. returned to the head of the table and sat down.

Looking directly at Indy he said, "You will have several direct supervisors that will determine your daily routines. You will listen and obey each of these people or you will be remanded back into custody and any and all privileges will be removed." Daniel Locke sr. looked down the length of the table at Indy with his arms crossed. "Do we have an understanding, Guardian?"

Indy nodded his head once, knowing full well that to deny his father now would weaken his position in the power struggle going on in the council's background.

Indy breathed a sigh of relief. He had let his father down, he could see that now. He had avoided accepting the responsibility of being a Guardian. It was easy, there was no effort, and he had just sat back and watched. Indy knew he should have taken a more proactive role in the community but he just didn't feel that he was ready. It was hard to believe any one of these people would respect or care about a seventeen year old kid. Now that Indy had a chance to calm down, he realized that his father was right. He had let passion rule his emotions and his anger had clouded his judgment. He had acted like a child. Indy knew he could have handled the situation a little more delicately, but at the same time, it was still nice to see Warren get a bit of his own medicine. He had to suppress a grin as he thought about Warren's busted nose.

His father's voice brought him back to the conversation that had started up around him.

"As to the other matters we need to discuss," he said. "The latest communications with the United States military have come in. It seems that a major skirmish has taken place in the waters just south of Hawaii. Reports include a highly detailed sighting of what is being referred to as a large floating Island mass, several thousand feet above the ocean's surface. The surveillance footage has been marked as TOP SECRET but a few photos have made their way into our possession. They are currently being analyzed by my team and will be available shortly."

The councillor to Canada, Tim Girard spoke up. He was a thin pale man in a black suit. "Is there anything else that we know about this floating island?"

Demetri Molotov, the Russian councillor nodded and cleared his throat importantly. "I have connections in the state department, they are sending us some satellite footage as we speak."

"Yes Demetri, we all know how important you are, but do we have anything to look at right now." Mark Sanders said, as he smiled in Demetri's direction. Mark was Britain's council and had a long-standing issue with the Russian.

"What we do have is this," Daniel said loudly as the men around the table started squabbling. Daniel nodded at his assistant who clicked on a projector.

Displayed on the far wall of the room was a scene straight out of a World War 3 movie. Smoking hulls of ships littered the water's surface and hundreds of jet fighters filled the skies. Several of the larger vessels were easily identifiable. The USS George Washington aircraft carrier at the foreground of the picture was smoking badly from a large crater in the middle of its flight deck.

"The battle you see displayed here was, for the most part, a chilling victory. The U.S. was able to turn back the Korean Army with minimal resistance. However, the damage seen in these photographs was not caused by the Koreans." His father paused a moment to let that sink in. "The destruction was caused by the aforementioned floating Island we now know to be Valhalla."

No one in the room made a sound. Even the hum of the projector seemed muted at the news of the awesome, destructive power of Valhalla. If Valhalla had that kind of firepower... Indy swallowed hard as he thought about what Valhalla could do to this little valley. Eden had nothing like the U.S.S. George Washington to protect it and if James was in control of the island, it was only a matter of time before he showed up here.

"Valhalla has since disappeared from sight. Advanced imaging and radar cannot locate it at this time." Daniel looked over to his son. "It has been confirmed by naval intelligence that the island's last trajectory puts it in line with Eden.

The E.D.T. has prepared several possible scenarios to work with. Doc believes that the briar wall that has risen around us may be a part of Eden's natural defenses. He also speculates that there may be other, unknown defenses Eden may have, that we are unaware of."

Daniel Locke sr. looked around the room at the men waiting on his every word.

"Going forward we will assume the worst," he said. "I have started work on an evacuation plan that will begin as soon as possible. The details of the plan will be on your desks later today. I remind all you gentlemen that the last thing we want is to panic the public. Eden may be secure against this incoming threat but I would rather be safe than sorry. We have had no contact with Adam and cannot be assured that the aurora surrounding this valley will be any kind of shield or deterrence to Valhalla."

"I can hardly believe that a scientist is a qualified individual to be leading a defense force of this nature. We need a strong presence to fill that role, a military presence." Demetri said as he puffed out his chest.

"Sit down Demetri." Mark said with a long sigh. "Just because you fought in the Afghanistan war doesn't mean you are a tactician. Geez, just look at the last time they let you touch an artifact. You almost burned down the dining hall."

Several of the councillors laughed hard at Demetri's expense. Demetri scowled at Mark but let a small smile creep across his face. "It was rather funny to see you scream like a little girl when that mop on your head started to burn as well."

Mark absently patted the toupee on his head to reassure himself it hadn't slipped. The others around him laughed even louder.

Daniel banged on the table once for quiet. "GENTLEMEN! This is serious, this is not something happening a million miles away, Valhalla is coming and we have to be ready."

The councillor's laughter quieted but none of them seemed to be put off by Daniel's harsh tone.

"The E.D.T. is stepping up its efforts to give us time to get the people of the castle to safety. Doc Hocking has put several new artifacts together that he believes may hinder any efforts to land on the beach. These artifact cannons are the combination of several different known artifacts that, when used simultaneously, cause a new and potentially volatile reaction. In the meantime, I urge each one of you to contact your homelands and request aid. We are in desperate need of any kind of military support or defensive operations. Thank you for your time gentlemen, we will resume deliberations after dinner. Hopefully by then we will have more information to share with you."

Daniel Locke nodded at his son before retreating into an office located at the back of the room. Around him, the councillors sat in silence for a few more moments before packing up their things and exiting the room.

Chapter 5 – Eden - My What?

The beach was a disaster. The once pristine sands were cluttered with bundles of wood, crates and workers struggling to build defensible structures.

During the council meeting the councillors had, in all their wisdom, decided that due to the ever-growing briar thorn barrier the weakest point of entry to the valley was through the beach. Several trenches had already been dug above the tide lines with deep pits scattered here and there. Sandbags were piled up into several bunkers and all along the ridge line concrete platforms were being built. The first of the platforms was already completed and a long metal tube was being affixed to a rotating control seat bolted into the cement.

Doc Hocking was overseeing this part of the defenses with the help of his science team. They had several crates of artifacts sitting nearby that they were piecing together. Doc was also Indy's supervisor of the day. Hocking had Indy running errands, digging ditches and any other menial job the man could think of. Currently Indy was working in the water, creating hidden obstacles below the surface.

"Hey stranger," Joslyn said as she wandered up the beach.

Indy had not noticed her approaching and was caught off guard. He had not forgotten the conversation he had overheard in the entertainment room.

Indy grunted his hello and bent back to his work. He was in the middle of stringing lines of barbed wire across the tide lines and burying long metal rods deep into the sand just under the water's surface. It was tiring, backbreaking work, but with his unbreakable skin, at least he didn't have to worry about snags and cuts. Indy was waist deep in the water and turned to look at Joslyn standing on the beach. The weather was cooling and she had dressed in a hoodie and jeans. Her crystalized hair sparkled in the sunlight and Indy's stomach started to churn with unease. This was going to be difficult. He couldn't directly confront her without admitting he had been eavesdropping. He also didn't want to let what he had heard just slide. So he decided now was not the time for this confrontation, tomorrow maybe he would sit down with her and have a long talk.

"I can't talk right now," Indy said without making eye contact. "Good old Doc is a real slave driver. I have to finish stringing this stuff before I can take a break. It is going to be awhile."

Joslyn looked slightly put off but nodded her head. "Okay, I will stop by a little later. I just wanted to talk to you about something but I guess it can wait."

"Sure, see ya in a bit then." Indy said as he ducked under the water to check on one of the long metal stakes. Underwater breathing was another one of the fantastic abilities his dragon tattoo had given him and when he came back up to the surface several minutes later, Joslyn was gone.

Frustrated, Indy stomped out of the water and over to where he had left his clothes and lunch box. The crate where he had hung his clothes up was still there but most of his stuff was gone. His lunch box was open and empty and the only piece of clothing left on the crate was his jeans. Looking around the beach, he searched for the practical joker he knew would be waiting to see his reaction. No one was around and no one was watching him. None of the usual suspects were around. No Jon, Allen, Warren or Thomas.

Puzzled Indy look around the immediate area as he pulled his jeans on, hoping to spot something that might have been misplaced. He did find something a little odd, on one piece of the crate, he thought he saw several small footprints. Looking a bit closer at the muddy tracks, he began to doubt what he actually saw. After all what kind of small creature has three toes?

"It must be some kind of bird," he thought to himself.

A small singsong voice called out from behind him. Startled again, Indy turned to see Adam sitting on a wooden crate just a few feet behind him.

"Adam, where did you come from? We haven't seen you in months." Indy asked as he walked over to the little boy who was wearing a three-piece suit. Adam looked exactly as he did the last time Indy had seen him in the tower.

"Hello Indy, I am sorry I haven't stopped by sooner but I have been occupied." Adam said with a bright cheery smile. "I had a little surprise in store for you, but to my disappointment the task could not be completed. It was just a little thank you for your efforts within the tower. I had hoped to leave it on your bed the night you became Guardian. I just want you to know I am still working on it."

Indy nodded absently at the mention of a gift. He had forgotten Adam mentioning it after his fight with Zeus. He looked down at Adam who was all smiles and curly blonde hair.

The little man was watching him carefully and after a few moments of silence said, "I trust you are feeling better, are the headaches still a problem?"

Indy shook his head. "The headaches are gone and I feel pretty good. I'm having a hard time sleeping lately, but I'm not very tired anymore."

"Ah, you are becoming more accustomed to your new ability," Adam said in his singsong voice. "Quite often a shield like yours takes a while for the body to get used to. It feeds off your own energies and emotions as it synchronizes to your body and can create situations where your mind might not be able to function properly. That is what causes the headaches and blackouts... pure exhaustion."

"However, the protection gained from the shield will never waiver while you remain under the protection of the aurora. You will find that your sleep patterns will lessen in time, a good night's sleep will only take a few hours." Adam smiled slightly and leaned forward on the crate, his little legs swinging back and forth.

A warmth at Indy's wrist made him look down at the dragon tattoo that was now wrapping itself around his forearm. The dragon looked up at him with its red eyes and smiled a wide toothy grin.

"You know there has been something bugging me about the whole dragon tattoo. James told me that part of his wish was to protect me, and that's how we both ended up with a shield."

Adam watched him closely with a slight grin on his face.

"Anyway, the part I found a little strange was the fact I found the dragon crystal in with my grandfather's old stuff. Is there any connection there? I mean did my grandfather know about how the artifacts and crystals worked?"

"No," Adam said with a slightly more serious expression on his face. "When James made the wish that summoned the shield charm, his oath to your mother enticed me to put the dragon crystal into your possession. It took quite a bit of effort to locate you and get the crystal into your hands. I had overheard your father requesting you retrieve several crystal objects from storage and I was able to place the crystal dragon among those items. The dragon crystal was never part of your grandfather's odd collection of crystal baubles. Once you passed into the tower's aurora, the crystal dragon activated upon contact with your skin.

A puzzled look crossed Indy's face and he said, "You are just full of answers today Adam. What gives? I don't mean to be rude, but the last time we talked, you said you couldn't answer questions that I didn't already know the answer to."

"Things have changed... Guardian." Adam said, as he looked around the beach. "Just the fact alone that you are Eden's Guardian gives you certain... rights."

"Rights? Like what exactly?" Indy asked excitement raising his voice slightly.

Adam hopped down from the crate and walked over to take Indy's hand.

"You are not going to like it, but again, we don't have much time for your questions. Come with me and I will let you in on a couple secrets before we need to run."

Adam began to lead Indy up the beach heading for the trail leading up the ridge. Adam was walking in silence and Indy patiently waited as they picked their way up the steep path.

"Do you remember when I told you the tower of Valhalla is coming?" Adam asked as they continued to walk and as Indy nodded Adam said, "Well the tower is already here."

Indy stopped to look down at the little boy's chubby little face. Adam looked like a small innocent child but there was a deep intelligence in his eyes. Those innocent eyes blinked at him as Indy's mind wrapped around the news. Indy looked up at the sky and all around the far horizon.

"I don't see any floating tower," Indy said.

"No, you can't see it just yet, but the tower is here. Your people have worked hard to prepare a defense for this valley, but ultimately it is useless. Valhalla is home to thousands of the world's best warriors and a depository for weapons that you have not even dreamed of yet. That is why the tower of Eden is hidden away, this valley will be overrun and there is nothing you can do to stop it."

"Is there anything at all we can do?" Indy asked as worry crossed his face.

"Valhalla itself is not evil," Adam said softly. "The people that control it now are confused and obsessed with power. In time, they may learn the error of their ways but now that Valhalla is active, Odin's main directive is to obtain and train warriors. For the time being that directive coincides with their quest for power."

A deep rumbling filled the air and the earth started to shake beneath their feet. Workers on the ridge stopped their work and looked around confused. Waves of wind pulsed down from above, whipping sand and debris around the beach. The rumbling noise turned a little hollow and then began to throb like a deep bass note resounding in Indy's chest. It was a slow beat but it was growing in strength. Several hundred feet outside of the Aurora California, the water was beginning to ripple and dance. With each throb, a massive pillar of water rose into the air. As the bass note got louder the water rose higher in response. The area affected was growing in size as well. Several other jets of water started to rise into the air from different spots in the ocean.

Indy looked up into the sky as a shadow crossed in front of the sun. A massive shape filled the air above the beach, easily ten miles wide but it was hard to make out, due to a large scattering of clouds. It was outside the Aurora California but as Indy looked a bit closer, he could tell something was rippling around the billowing cloudbank.

"It's got an aurora too?" Indy asked.

"Yes, the aurora is a side effect of the power generation. No aurora, no power, no floating island." Adam looked into the sky at the looming landmass. "Don't worry about our little valley, the tower and the great tree are safe. Your friends and family however... well that gets a bit complicated."

"Complicated?" Indy asked

Adam nodded, "I can't protect everyone from this threat. My powers are not that extensive. If it comes down to a battle, people could get hurt. You wanted to know what you could do to help, you must find a way to remove whoever is influencing Odin."

People were running from the beach as debris continued to whip around. Sirens had started wailing in the distance as the castle alerted everyone to the possible danger. Confused people were running back and forth adding to the chaos.

"Take care Indy," Adam said, his face growing sad. "Take care of your friends, they will need your help in the near future. As I said before, we both need to run."

A loud whistling filled the air as two black streaks came rushing into the aurora and over the beach. Two large ravens flashed by overhead as Indy pulled Adam down to the ground. The black birds curled around the ridge and flashed back across the beach and out of the aurora.

Indy picked himself up off the ground and then helped Adam to his feet.

"What were those things?" Indy asked as he stared out across the water.

"Valkyries." Adam said shaking his head. "They claim those fallen in battle that Odin deems worthy. It is how Valhalla builds its army. Beware Indy, the battle comes, watch over your friends. I must go now but do not fear, I will see you again soon."

Adam gave Indy a little hug before running back down the beach and out into the water. His little curly head bobbed once and then disappeared below the surface. Indy watched for a few more moments before turning back towards the castle. He needed to go see his father before the coming battle, if this whole defense was a farce, they needed to start the evacuation. He also needed to grab a fresh change of clothes on the way.

When Indy ran into the castle's council room he found the place was in chaos, councillors were panicking and tempers were flaring. Demetri and Mark were in a heated discussion that had several other councillors vocally taking one side or the other. Maps were tacked to the walls and a projector was broadcasting multiple camera angles of the beach and valley.

Sam Brown, who was Zeus's replacement as Captain of the security team, stood to one side of the room. Sam wore a dark blue guard's uniform and a pair of black sunglasses. The man wasn't as big as you might expect for the captain of the guard, but he was solid. Sam nodded at Indy as he came running into the room and motioned to a door at the back of the chamber. A slight smile crossed Sam's face as Indy walked past, heading to the door. That was the thing Indy liked most about Sam. The guy was all business but he was still friendly. To Sam everything had to be by the book. Rules were in place for a reason. Step out of line and Sam would be the first person to let you know about it. The little incident with Warren was in the past and that little smile from Sam assured Indy, that in the past was where it would stay.

The door at the back of the room was closed and inside, Indy could hear muffled voices in another heated verbal debate. Indy raised his hand to knock but before he could, the door flew open. Doc Hocking came striding out of the room, his face was sullen and his grey hair a tangled mess. The white lab coat he wore was wrinkled and dirty but the smile that was plastered across his wrinkled face was chilling. Doc didn't even acknowledge Indy's presence as he moved past and spoke quietly with Sam. Indy watched as the two men continued to talk as they left the room.

"Junior?" His father's voice called from within the room.

Indy turned to see his father smiling at him from behind a large oak desk. Daniel Locke sr. looked impeccable in his tailored business suit and sleek brown hair as he motion his son to sit in a large cushioned chair.

"Sit down Junior, I am glad you came in when you did. We are really past due for a talk."

"I am sorry about the whole Warren thing. I know I..." Indy said cautiously.

"Don't worry about it, I know what kind of punk that Hocking kid is. The apple doesn't fall far from the tree in my opinion. If Doc didn't have so many supporters on the council, I could have got you off a bit easier." Daniel shook his head at an absent thought. "That isn't what I want to talk to you about though."

Indy studied his father a little closer as Daniel shuffled some papers around the massive desk. Indy recognized the nervous energy right away, his father never fidgeted, whatever was on his mind was something big.

"What's up D?" Indy asked trying to lighten the sour mood descending into the room.

His father's face brightened with a quick smile. "Ok Junior, I am going to be straight with you. I made a promise to you not to keep any more secrets, so here goes. I swear to you I just found out. I may have suspected things, but I didn't know for sure until earlier this morning."

"Dad, just spit it out already." Indy insisted.

"Okay, but I wish I could share this with you at a better time. If I would have only known before all this..." Daniel Locke swept his arms out wide motioning around the room.

"Dad, seriously, just spit it out." Indy said as he leaned forward eager to hear his father's words.

Daniel Locke sr. stopped shuffling the papers and looked at his son. "It's about James."

Indy held his breath.

"James is... your brother. He is my son." Daniel said in a rush as his shoulders slumped and he sat back to watch Indy's reaction.

Indy fell back into the cushioned chair mouth agape. In stunned silence, he stared at his father. It took a few moments to sink in, even then, the news struck him with a resounding slap.

"Brother?" Indy asked, not believing it.

Daniel nodded. "Sasser brought me the proof. Before James left, I had Sasser working on the backgrounds of everyone in the castle. He noticed a few things didn't check out and began investigating deeper." Daniel nudged the folder on his desk. "Sasser is a very thorough man. He dug up a few things I would have preferred people not to know. I think your mom might have been protecting James as well. Sasser didn't find anything connecting the two of them, but when I look back, there were times that Jolie went out her way for him.

Indy was silent as he watched his father. He could tell the man had mixed feelings. Happy at the news of a son and yet devastated by the secrecy of it all.

Daniel smiled at his son and explained, "It happened before I met your mom. A business trip to Laos, Korea. I was young and in a strange new place. Indy, trust me, I had no idea that James was my son. I had no idea I had even fathered a child." Daniel Locke sr. looked straight into Indy's eyes. The man needed the comfort and assurance of a son.

"I believe you dad." Indy said with a slight nod of his head.

They shared a smile as Daniel began shuffling the papers again.

"There was one other item Sasser uncovered." His father's voice faltered. "It seems that a few years ago when we had a traitor in our midst... Well it looks like James was the one responsible for our product leaking to the Chinese. It turns out that the Yakuza brokered the deal and may have siphoned off other intelligence and money we are still not aware of."

"Why..." Indy's voice broke and he had to swallow before he could speak again. "...did he hide from us?"

"That," his father said. "I don't know. What I do know, is that the three dead Chinese soldiers we have buried out back, all have Yakuza tattoo's all over their bodies." Daniel flipped open the folder and spread several autopsy mug shots across the table. "Whoever is behind these men had a lot of power and ambition, a stealth plane full of soldiers doesn't come cheap."

Indy looked at the photographs of the dead men and shivered. It was a terrible, freaky way to die. Doc had told him previously about their cause of death. The three of them all had had their necks broken when their chutes had pulled them from their plane after it was shot down over the Pacific.

A knock sounded on the door and a small thin man entered the room when Daniel said, "Enter."

It was one of his father's new assistants. "Sir, the cloud system is starting to break up, we have a clearer image now."

"Thank you Cecil." His father said and rose from the desk. "Come on Junior, let's see what big bad wolf is knocking on our door.

Indy followed his father back into the council room. The room was still and staring at the images being cast on the projection screen. On the main screen was a rocky island filled with towers, arches and large square buildings. Each building was made of a dark stone and the entire island was wrapped in a familiar circle of shimmering air.

Indy spoke first, "You have got to be joking, another castle?"

"No joke Guardian," a voice called from behind him. Indy turned to look at the man who had spoken. It had been the Russian councillor, Demetri. Demetri was almost a mirror image of Indy's father. Fit and polished in a tailored blue business suit. Only their eyes and hair were different, Demetri had black hair and black penetrating eyes.

"That castle isn't a hunting lodge, it is built for battle." Demetri said, with a hint of envy in his voice. Demetri walked forward and began to point out features Indy might have missed or overlooked. "As you can see, that is no castle, it is a fortress."

Daniel Locke took his son by the shoulder and led him to the door.

"Junior, I want you to head up to the roof, I have assigned you and your friends to be our own little air force."

Indy looked at his father with a sense of dread obvious on his face. "What? Dad..."

"I know about the heights thing, but you and Jon are our best pilots. Doc had another one of those A.G.P.s things, you know, the anti-gravity sleds, hidden away in that plant of his along with a few other unnamed secrets. I really should be upset with the man but his little private stash of artifacts might just give us a little breathing room. It took some doing to pry that thing from him but in the end, our best plans included a stealthy sneak attack. We need you two on those sleds. I left your instructions with Joslyn, she will be up there to assist you both. Now get going, and be safe."

"That's not it dad," Indy said as he put a hand on his father's shoulder. "I just spoke to Adam down on the beach."

The chaos and clatter around the room abruptly stopped as soon as Adam's name was mentioned. Indy could feel the eyes of everyone in the room staring at him and waiting on his every word.

"What did he say?" Daniel demanded. "We haven't seen him in months, since the tower disappeared."

"He said that... that..." Indy looked around the room at the hopeful looks on everyone's face. This was going to be hard. "Adam said that our defenses won't be enough. We need to move as many people out of the castle and other buildings as we can."

For a second everyone in the room held their breath. Then the room went into a frenzy of activity with Daniel Locke sr. directing it with a loud booming voice.

"You heard the Guardian," he said. "Evacuate the castle, make sure you call down to the hydro plant as well. I don't care if Doc has made it his H.Q. or not, get those people out of the building. Cedric, I want you to take a Razor out to the Believer's compound. Tell them what is going on and make them aware of the situation."

Indy watched in amazement as his father began his evacuation plans. Assigning each councillor a task and ushering them out the door. When the room was finally cleared of everyone but the two of them, his father turned to face him.

"Junior, we need to buy some time to get everyone to safety. I need you to do whatever you can to slow down anything Valhalla throws our way. I have a plan in place that will safeguard everyone, but I can't tell you just yet. I cannot risk telling anyone who might be captured where I am going to hide all these people. When the defenses break, I want you and Jon to get back to the roof of the castle. Joslyn and I will meet you there and then I will take the three of you to the safe room."

"Okay Dad, I will do what I can." Indy said as a sense of foreboding swept over him. He grabbed his dad in a fierce hug. "Stay safe dad. I think Adam will look out for us, but he seemed worried. Something bad is going to happen, I just know it."

"Junior... don't worry about me, you have a job to do. I expect that from now on, you might take the whole Guardian thing a little more seriously, okay?"

Indy nodded slowly, "Okay dad, I will, I promise."

"Good," Daniel said as he punched Indy's arm. "Let's get you suited up. Your friends are waiting."

Chapter 6 – Eden - Air Force

Jon and Joslyn were waiting on the roof of the castle by the time Indy arrived already dressed in his black flight suit with his helmet tucked under one arm. Jon was Indy's mirror image with one slight exception, he was wearing a gun holster under one arm.

"What's with the gun Jon?" Indy asked.

Guns were common around the castle but usually only the guards carried them openly.

Jon shrugged, "It's my dad's. He wanted me to have a bit more protection out there, you know, just in case."

Joslyn spoke up just then, maybe noticing Indy's lack of attention towards her. "Indy, is everything okay? You seem a little... off."

Off was a good way to describe it. Between the news flash about James being his brother and Joslyn... well, he still wasn't sure about her. So instead of broaching the subject with Joslyn, Indy told them both about James.

"Brother?" Jon and Joslyn said in unison.

"Step brother." Indy corrected.

"The same guy who shot your dad?" Joslyn asked.

"The same," Indy sighed.

Things were not getting any easier, just being near Joslyn made his heart ache and even the conversation he had overheard was taking a backseat in his mind as he looked at her. But now just wasn't the time to get to the bottom of it. Anything could happen in the next couple of hours and he wanted a clear mind, just in case things went bad.

A series of loud noises pierced the air like a snapping branch. In the distance, the floating island looked like it was dropping large chunks of rocks into the ocean below. Several dark shapes hit the water causing large plumes to splash skyward. The three of them raced to the edge of the roof to get a better look.

Joslyn took up the bumblebee telescope and pointed it towards the ocean.

"Hang on, just focusing... oh my god, those weren't rocks, they were ships!" She yelled.

Several of the ships had risen to the surface and were sprouting long oars from their sides. Their black hulls were hard to see against the dark ocean, but it was all too obvious where they were heading.

Sirens went off all over the castle and the walkie-talkie at Joslyn's hip started to chatter. "Battle stations, battle stations, this is not a drill.

All personnel proceed to their designated stations."

"You boys better get strapped in." Joslyn said, motioning to the two sleek black A.G.P.s sitting on the far side of the roof. "I put Doc's homemade AA bombs in the backpacks. The blue bag has Jon's and Indy gets the red one."

"AA bombs?" Indy asked. "What are they?"

"Oh man, I'm sorry," Jon said. "I was supposed to get you up to speed on our part of all this."

Jon shrugged helplessly, and pointed at the beach down below.

"They want us to be utility players. Doc made up a bunch of anti artifact bombs. It's some kind of acid that destroys an artifact and most other things on contact. He made two different types of bottle bombs. Both are in plastic water bottles because the acid will not eat through them. One type has a concussion grenade attached to it and the other has a high explosive grenade."

Jon looked at Indy with a small smile, "Guess which one is in the red bag."

Indy rolled his eyes and crossed his arms as Jon continued, "The grenades help to scatter the liquid so you want to make sure to detonate just above your target for maximum effect. Just a couple of drops are all it takes to take out most artifacts. We can't use a spray system like the guys on the ground because the A.G.P.s are artifacts after all."

"I am going to relay targets to you via your helmet's radio system," Joslyn said as she reached for Indy's hand.

She took him by the hand and led them both to the sleds. "You guys be careful, if you run into any problems, get back to the castle. Your dad wants us to meet back here when we are done. If you can't make it back here, head to Hank's place. He isn't taking any part of this mess but he will shelter anyone who needs help."

When they reached the sleds, Jon slipped into his but before Indy could do the same, Joslyn's frost covered fingers tightened around his hand. She turned Indy to face her and looked deep into his eyes.

"I know something's wrong Indy. You might not want to tell me right now but when you get back, will you promise to tell me then?"

Indy nodded and gave her a half-hearted lopsided grin. Joslyn gave him a long hug and then abruptly pushed him towards the A.G.P.

"Seeya flyboy," she said as she tapped his black helmet. "Try to keep the channel clear unless you see something important you need to report."

Indy slipped the red pack across his back and tucked into the sled. The black helmet drowned out the sirens still going off around the castle. Indy gave a quick nod to Jon when he was set. Together they lifted off the roof and descended to ground level. Indy's stomach heaved as they dropped over the edge but it was nothing he couldn't handle. Maybe he could get used to this after all, as long as he didn't go too high up.

Once at ground level the sleds rocketed away from the castle heading out across the soccer fields and to the north. Jon took the lead as they raced just below treetops. Once they reached the aurora near the quarry road, they swung around and followed the edge of shimmering lights back to the coast.

"Ok Indy, here is the deal." Jon's voice crackled as it came through his helmets radio system. "It's our job to be forward scouts until we get our orders. I am going to head up to the cloud level and watch from there. Doc said that the A.G.P.'s are waterproof, so if you want to head out into the surf, you can keep an eye from the water."

Indy nodded and gave Jon a thumbs up. Jon returned the gesture and gave his sled a burst of speed. The sleek black sled twisted and turned as it climbed up into the air. Jon had really mastered the art of flying, Indy thought as he watched his friend disappear into the clouds. Indy kicked his own sled into motion and slid along at ground level until he reached the ocean. The mist from the pounding waves clouded his visor as he skimmed along the wave tops and as the A.G.P. passed over the water, it raised little fountains in its wake.

Indy stopped once he neared the edge of the aurora and hovered in place. Looking back down the coastline to the castle, he could see the immense floating island causing the same ripples in the water below its rocky bottom. From this angle, he could see the two separate auroras clearly. Both were identical in color and stretched from the ground and up into the sky. Inside the Valhalla aurora, the ocean frothed and surge like rain dancing on a drum. He could see little else moving inside the other aurora. However, on his side of the Aurora California it was another story. At the top of the cliff near the castle, he could see people scurrying about preparing for the worst. It looked like the castle defense team was in place and waiting for whatever was about to happen.

A hollow boom echoed out from the island, rolling across the ocean like a fist of air. Sand and debris rippled off the beach as the sonic wave hit. Even the great white tree swayed from the blast of air, several of its leaves popping and rising into the air as they were loosened from their branches. Indy watched the bottom of the Valhalla Island as several more dark shapes dropped free and plunged down into the ocean. This time the shapes dropping from the bottom of the island were larger, much larger. Huge plumes of water rose from the ocean as the shapes hit. They disappeared from view for only a moment before bobbing back up to the surface. Long sticks appeared from both sides of each of the shapes and started to propel them forward, towards the beach.

Joslyn's voice echoed in his helmet. "We've got more ships in the water, these ones look bigger though, looks like some kind of troop carrier. You guys stay put for now. But be ready to move, this is it."

The long ships paddled out from under Valhalla's shadow moving quickly. The vessels had entered the space in between auroras and were paddling hard towards the Aurora California. The significance of the trek was not lost on Indy.

"Looks like they have more apples or something," he said into his mic.

Eating one of Adam's golden apples was the only way Indy knew of to escape an aurora without turning into a crystal statue.

"Roger that Indy," Jon said in reply.

The smaller vessels breached the Aurora California first and the second they crossed into Eden, began spewing a thick white smoke. In moments, the entire beachfront was covered in a thick white fog. The fog spread its way across the water like a forest fire and eventually the fog had Indy wrapped in its dense embrace. Indy lost sight of the other larger ships in the dense fog, but he knew they were still coming. A soft rhythmic sound started to echo off the water and got steadily louder as shadows started approaching through the fog. The beating drums grew louder and louder as the shadows came closer. Indy could hear a muted song coming across the water, it was strange and eerie, but he couldn't make out the words. Sounds of the oars splashing into and out of the water, alerted Indy to the ships proximity. Then he spotted the shadows of the largest ships coming at him from the fog.

The ships passed through Eden's aurora without slowing. Each one was about twenty feet in length and looked more like a submarine than a ship. Ten long poles swept back and forth in the water propelling the boats forward quickly. The first in line was almost to the beach when it hit the traps Indy had driven into the ocean floor. The other boats came to a stop behind the first vessel as hatches popped at the rear of all the ships. Indy watched as a man poked his head out of the nearest hatch to look around. He was wearing a thick military style helmet and was carrying a long machine gun that he propped on the ship's hull in front of him. Several of the other ships had gunners in place as well.

Nothing else moved for minutes as the standoff dragged on and the fog continued to swirl across the water and out onto the beach. The beach was clear of all people and the dark ships in the water stood silent. Without warning, large sections of the boats split open from the front and a wave of soldiers came pouring out, running down long planks that they extended out into the water.

For the most part, the underwater barbwire traps proved useless. The problem was that the first group of the soldiers disembarking from the ships wore artifact armour. The armoured warriors simply tore through the barbed wire on their way to the sandy beach. The familiar looking dark grey armour flashed in the sunlight as the men reached the beach and unslung assault rifles of every sort. At the head of each group of men was a single person holding a strange bowl shaped object. The first carrier stopped just feet onto the beach and buried the bowl down into the sand. As the man stepped away, a burst of lightning followed and a large wall flashed into existence. The wall was electric blue and about ten feet long and ten feet high.

A split second after the wall appeared a boom echoed from the cliffs above. A burst of color flowed from the cliffs like a rainbow and smacked into the wall with a muffled thud. Flames and sparks ricocheted off the wall in a thousand different directions.

"Whoa," Jon said as he marvelled at the display. "That must be one of the firework cannons Doc was building."

"Warren was supposed to wait for the signal before firing." Joslyn complained over the radio.

With that explosion, the battle was on in earnest. Tracer fire lit from the hatchways of the ships as even more men poured out. Although the newest group of men were dressed in military fatigues, none wore the artifact armour the first group had worn.

In response, the E.D.T. team on the cliff rained mortar fire down from above. Loud explosions rocked the beach and sand was blown in every direction. Indy watched as more bowls were carried from the ships and placed in an ever-growing series of defensive shelters. One of the first armoured Valhalla soldiers to come around the electric blue wall was greeted with another blast of fireworks from one of the three cannons stationed up on the ridge. The man in the armour was hurled back into the ocean by the explosive force of the shot. The beach broke into chaos as the battle raged and the explosions rang.

"Jon, Indy," Joslyn said. "I have your assignments. Jon, they want you to hit the first shield wall. Indy, they want you to hit the ship closest to the beach. Once you drop your bombs, clear away and wait for your next orders."

"Roger, Roger," they replied and started towards their targets.

Jon was there first, dropping fast from the sky, he dropped the bottle bomb at the base of the wall. After dropping the bomb, Jon skimmed across the sand and blasted back up into the clouds. Seconds after the bottle bomb hit, the concussion grenade went off. Electricity danced around the wall and the barrier fizzled out of existence.

"Direct hit," Joslyn said.

Indy's run was a little less visual but still impressive. His A.G.P. raced just above the waves and rose up to the ships hatch level as it slowed. The man firing the machine gun from the hatch was wearing thick headgear and didn't hear the thrump, thrump, thrumpt of the sled as it approached. The AA bottle dropped from Indy's hand and bounced off the man's back before rolling down into the hatch. Indy sped away as a second later an explosion rocked the boat. The gunner was tossed from the hatch and out into the water as smoke poured from the now empty hatchway.

"Nice one Indy!" Joslyn complimented.

With the main defensive wall gone, the firework cannons began to pound the incoming soldiers relentlessly. Soldiers were tossed like rag dolls around the beach as the fireworks blossomed.

A whistling sound echoed over the water as two dark ravens raced out from the thick clouds of fog overhead. Indy watched the closest one flash by and saw in its claws, a long silver spear. As the ravens weaved through the air and up the cliffs, they released their silver spears. With minimal noise, the two spears thudded into the ground at the base of two firework cannons.

"They missed the gunners," Joslyn reported as the two ravens streaked back over the battlefield and back out into the mist.

Another louder noise filled the air as something from the floating island of Valhalla started to glow. Seconds later, massive bolts of lightning fell from the sky and arced into the two silver spears. The impact was immense and blew apart the cannons and anything else near them for twenty feet. As the smoke cleared, only the two silver spears remained. Each spear glowed a brilliant bright white amongst the charred debris of the cannons.

The devastation left them all speechless for several heartbeats. Indy was the first to act. Turning the A.G.P., he raced up the beach and along the cliffside until he reached the closest spear. Spinning the sled over onto its side, he was able to reach down and pull the white-hot spear from the earth. In his hands, the spear gave off a familiar warm sensation, the same warmth he felt when he had touched Adam's hand. Indy lifted the sled higher off the ground as he looked for a target.

A grouping of soldiers caught Indy's eye and he found one person that stood out from among the rest. It was the only person on the beach not in artifact armour, or even in military fatigues. The man was dressed in a black outfit and wore a strange metal helmet on his head. The helmet seemed to give off a black smoky aura as the man walked up the beach. Everything about the helmet was black. It had long sweeping curved horns and a faceplate that looked like a thousand sharp teeth. Even the eye sockets of the helmet seemed to radiate blackness. Even though the black form was walking among the soldiers, none of them came within feet of the man.

Indy eyed the man and then angled the A.G.P. onto an intercept course. The spear was light in his hand and its warmth gave him a reassuring feeling as the sled rocketed down the cliff's steep slope. The sled danced in its flight, bobbing and weaving in the air, creating a hard target to hit. The man in black stopped and watched as Indy came closer. The spear in Indy's hand started to whistle in the fast moving wind. The whistling drew everyone's eye and Indy threw the spear as hard as he could when he was finally in range. The silver missile struck the ground between a pair of black combat boots. The eyes of the helmet looked from the silver spear to Indy and then back again before raising a hand in a gesture Indy instantly recognized.

"James!" Indy shouted.

Stepping over the spear, James continued up the beach at a slow walk. All the other soldiers around the spear ran for cover. Seconds later the lightning came again. Several of the slower soldiers were caught in its blast and were flung across the sand.

Anger swept over Indy like nothing he had ever felt before. The rage inside Indy was all-consuming and his vision tunnelled until he could only see one thing, James. As his vision tunnelled, Indy's hearing became muted as well. Only his heart and breath sounded in his ears as Indy swung the A.G.P. around and aimed it at the man's back. Seconds before he reached James an impact blasted into him. Fireworks scattered over his body and the sled as one of the firework cannons blew him from the sky. The forward momentum of the A.G.P. carried Indy bouncing and rolling across the sand only to come to rest at James's black combat boots. The sled however disintegrated into carbon dust.

Indy bounced to his feet and tore the helmet from his head. Facing James, he curled his hands into fists and prepared to fight his stepbrother.

"A moment Indy." James said in a calm but demanding voice as he held a hand up to forestall the Indy's attack.

Only a few feet separated the siblings as James reached up to take his helmet off. The black mist around James disappeared as the helmet came off. Under the helmet, an odd grin was plastered over James's face as he regarded Indy.

"I take it you and father have already found out my little secret?"

Indy could only grunt in reply, his anger was boiling and he could only contain himself so much.

"Look Indy, you don't understand, things are complicated." James said but stopped abruptly as he noticed the soldiers who had run away from the spear were already coming back.

The soldiers surrounded the two siblings in a ring, guns drawn. Then the look on James's face changed, and was replaced by an angry light that burned deep within his eyes. The black helmet in his hands was violently tugged back onto his head. The voice that came from within the helmet was eerie and malevolent.

"Seize him," James said and pointed at Indy. "Lock him in one of the ship's holds until I have time to deal with him, personally."

Hands were reaching out to grab Indy before he could even take a step forward. Just as he was spun around to face the ships, another explosion stuck him. A solid burst of cannon fireworks hit him in the back, a direct hit on the red backpack he was still wearing. The resulting explosion was massive, the grenades inside the bag exploded and acid was sprayed everywhere. Indy's body was blown clear off the beach and out into the ocean's surf.

At the edge of consciousness, Indy could only watch what happened next. His shield must have started to fade or began to use his bodies own energies to maintain itself. Indy could feel his strength fading and his head began to sag, nodding into the water.

James screamed in anger. Turning from the destruction wreaked by the explosion, he pointed at the cannon responsible and huffed a command through the helmet.

In response to the command, the two ravens streaked from the mist and raced over the beach. It just so happened that the gunner of the cannon that had interrupted James, was none other than Warren Hocking. Warren was realigning the cannon for another shot when the large black ravens struck. The guards surrounding the cannon had no time to react. Plucking Warren from the gunner seat the large ravens dragged him through the air and back to the beach where they dropped him in front of James.

James hit Warren with several heavy kicks to the teenager's ribs. The thuds echoed across the beach and the young man screamed in pain. Darkness seemed to seep from James as he reached down to lift Warren from the ground. Lifting him into the air by the throat, James started to yell at him.

"Indy is mine to deal with as I will. You shall never touch him again." James's voice turned deep and menacing as he reached into a bag at his hip.

He produced a shining golden orb from the bag and in one smooth motion, crushed it into Warren's chest. James tossed Warren away like a piece of garbage and stood over the young man, as he lay crumpled on the beach. Warren had landed hard but was making his way to a kneeling position as tendrils of mist started radiating from the spot where the golden orb had been crushed. A layer of frost began creeping across Warren's body, leaving a thick crystal residue in its wake.

The light glistening off Warren's statue was the last thing Indy saw before his head finally sank below the waves. He had no more energy left to even hold his head up and numbness crept over him as the surf pulled him away from the beach.

Something had Indy by the shoulders and was lifting him slowly from the water. Indy noticed a strange pendant hanging from his neck and dark skinned arms wrapped around his chest.

A soft voice was calling to him, lulling him. "Be calm young hero, your journey is just beginning."

The voice above him was calm and soothing. Indy's mouth tingled, as he tasted a lingering sweetness on his lips. As he passed through the Aurora California, Indy felt only numbness as he rose higher into the air. A sense of weightlessness filled him as he was lifted higher and higher. The beach was spreading out below him and he could see everything from this height. There was Jon, racing along the coast on his A.G.P., probably looking for Indy's body in the water. James and Warren were further away but Indy could see them easily from this perspective.

James was leaning over Warren's statue yelling something Indy could not quite hear. With a shove, James turned Warren's statue to face the Hydro plant in the distance. Once the statue was facing the plant, James pulled a flask from under his black shirt. Uncapping it, James rubbed some of the liquid from the flask over his fingers and in one rough move, slapped Warren across one side of his face.

Instantly the crystal covering that section of Warren's face melted away, leaving smooth unbroken skin and a wide blinking eye. Moving to stand where the uncovered eye could see him, James bent over Warren's statue and smiled. With a gesture, he motioned at the hydro plant.

"Now," James said, raising his voice to the sky.

Even at this distance, Indy heard the voice echoing over the water.

A ripple of power sang through the air around him and the hydro plant exploded in a flash of bright light. Waves of energy washed over the beach as the plant and everything inside it was vaporized. When the light faded, nothing was left but a smoking pile of debris. Without looking back, James made his way off the beach and towards the castle in the distance. There was nothing left to slow his progress as the remaining defenders simply broke and ran.

Indy lifted his head from the scene on the beach to see who or what was carrying him higher into the air.

As he looked up, he found a dark pair of female eyes looking down at him. White feathers circled her long black hair in a crown.

For some reason Indy couldn't find a reason to care where this angel was taking him. The numbness had spread over his body and had begun to creep into his mind.

"Don't worry my little hero, you are safe. I am a Valkyrie and you have been chosen. The life you have known is now over and a new one will begin shortly."

Feathered wings were beating around them as the pair rose even higher in the air. There was a strange rocky mass in front of them, appearing out of the clouds. It seemed to hover in the air and for some strange reason, Indy could not seem to remember what it was called.

Chapter 7 – Valhalla - The White Valkyrie

The Valkyrie soared higher and higher, until they were level with a rocky island that seemed to appear out of the clouds. At the center of the island was a massive group of buildings, stacked one on top of the other, the largest of them being a tower made of stone.

During the flight, Indy blacked out several times, but when he passed over a high stone wall, his mind cleared a bit and he began to pick out features of the massive fortress and the forest surrounding it. Scattered across the island were many types of trees, but it was the largest tree that caught and held his eye. It was pure white and towered above the others. Its leaves were pure gold and shone like gems in the sunlight. The massive tree reminded Indy of something he could not quite put his finger on.

The Valkyrie's white feathered wings stopped beating and stretched out to either side as she began to glide down towards the buildings. As she passed over the thick squat buildings, men on the ground and rooftops lifted their heads to watch the Valkyrie's approach. Some even raised a hand in greeting as she winged past.

With a sudden rush of wings, Indy was deposited on a stone roof. In front of him stood another squat stone building with an open wooden door. The Valkyrie folded her wings and landed softly behind him. Taking Indy's hand, she led him inside the building.

"This is your home now young Hero. Everything you need will be provided, the servants of Odin will see to it. I must go." The Valkyrie smiled cheerfully as she turned to leave.

Indy came out of his mind numbing daze and started to realize this was all way too real. This was not some dream and he was not dead.

"What are you, are you an angel?" He asked.

The vision with wings spoke in a smooth and strong voice. "No, I am no angel, little hero, I am a Valkyrie."

At the word Valkyrie, the white wings on her back rose a little higher above her shoulders and ruffled with pride.

"It is our job to save the greatest heroes on the cusp of death and deliver them here, to Valhalla."

Indy reached for the woman as she turned, grabbing for a wrist.

"Wait, are you saying I was dying?" Indy asked.

The Valkyrie's wings opened slightly forcing Indy to release his hold and pushed him a small distance away.

"You had been defeated by your enemies and lay broken and fading in the waters below when I scooped you into my arms and carried you here."

Indy thought for a moment and tried to clear the fuzz from his memory. "You saved me... I remember, an explosion, my head slipping under the water. Indy's eyes focused on the woman's wings. The wings that had lifted him high above a raging battle and out of danger. "Thank you..." he said, pausing to wait for the Valkyrie's name.

Her eyes flashed when she spoke, "I am Kara."

The crown of white feathers around her head seemed to brighten when she spoke, not quite glowing, but definitely more enhanced than it was a second ago.

"Kara." Indy let the name hang on his lips savouring it for a lasting moment. "I need your help, Kara, I can't seem to remember anything. I get these weird pictures flashing in my head, but I don't know what they mean. I am not even sure what my name is... I think it is Indy, but everything is so blurry."

Kara looked closely at him and her dark eyes softened just a little.

"That is good little hero, your old life is dead. You have been born anew. Your actions and deeds will provide you a new name when it is time."

The Valkyrie stepped closer to him and raised a hand to his face.

"It is odd you remember your old name though, none of the others have remembered theirs. I think you might be destined to become a great one."

Kara smiled as she brushed his cheek and turned for the door. Before she left, she had one more piece of advice.

"Go see Gammon, he is our blacksmith, he will get you started on your path to glory."

With that, her white wings lifted her into the air and quickly out of sight.

Indy watched her go, feeling a strange loss in his heart. He turned from the doorway and began to search the small building. On a table, he found a long knife, its hilt bound in leather. On impulse, he sat down at the table and began to slide the blade along its wooden surface. The knife was sharp and within seconds, he was looking down at one word carved into the tabletop. INDY. His pulse quickened as he looked down at the name. Something within him responded to the word.

So he said it aloud. "Indy."

The name reverberated in his mind, and something clicked. It was his name, he couldn't remember anything else, but at least he could remember his own name.

A voice spoke from the doorway. "Ah, welcome hero."

Indy turned to see a large man filling the doorway. Shiny silver armour covered every inch of the man. Through the man's helmet, Indy could see the warrior had long blonde hair and a single blue eye. In place of the other eye was brilliant red ruby. The man raised a metal covered hand in greeting.

"My name is Gammon Windsong," he said. "The white Valkyrie told me of your arrival. She asked that I take special care of you. I don't know who you are stranger, but I think the white lady is rather fond of you."

The man walked into Indy's house carrying a large rucksack that clinked when he set it down.

"I brought a few things to get us started, you won't be trained in weapons for a while yet, so a sword can wait."

Gammon reached into the bag and started pulling armour from its depths.

"You will find that as you win duels and trials you will be rewarded with newer equipment. As a general rule the more decorated the piece, the more prized it is."

Indy looked at the pile of armour growing larger on his floor. He had no clue how to put any of it on. Gammon however paid him little attention. The bearded man admired a metal helmet before throwing it back into the pile.

A sudden thought came to Indy. "Why do you call me hero?" he asked.

Gammon looked up from the growing pile of equipment and smiled. "We are all heroes here lad. That is why the Valkyrie's choose us. Don't ask what ya did though, I don't know myself. Odin collects warriors for a day he calls Ragnarok. On that day, the Halls of the Brave will open up and we shall pour forth onto the world below. Until that day, we train."

Gammon flung a thick grey metal helmet his way. "Try that on, it should be a good start for you."

Dropping the helmet on his head Indy found it to be a perfect fit.

"The rest of this stuff is all adjustable and should fit without any problem. Get dressed and then come over to the Hall of Heroes. We have to get a feel for your skills, young warrior."

Gammon turned to leave but was stopped by a question from Indy. "How exactly do I get to the Halls of the Heroes?"

"Aye... well I guess I need to help ya there. You will have to forgive me, I am a blacksmith not a tour guide. Balder is the one who should be greeting our new members. But alas, Balder decided to follow the strangers to ground level. That man always wants to be in the middle of things."

"Strangers?" Indy asked.

"The soldiers Odin has allowed to stay in Valhalla... for the time being. A group of soldiers parachuted onto Valhalla a few months ago, led by an old grey stick in the mud by the name of Tapper. Odin allowed them to stay, if any one of their number passed the trial of the Guardian."

"Trial of the Guardian?" Indy was sure he had heard of the trials somewhere before. His mind was ringing with memories that would not form completely.

"Aye," Gammon said. "The trial is Odin's way of selecting a worthy warrior to lead his forces, when Ragnarok comes. The warrior that wins is granted great powers, and greater reign of Valhalla. It was our newest Guardian that brought Valhalla here today. He said it would be a field test, an exercise to help prepare the army for the coming battles."

Indy felt a stirring in his belly and a desire growing in his mind he could not explain. It was as if a fire had been lit inside him.

"How does one enter the trials of the Guardian?"

Gammon turned to stare at Indy with his one good eye. "The trials are a serious affair boy," he said as he examined Indy a little closer. "One does not simply pass or fail the trial. It is a matter of life and death, only the living pass. If you lose the trial, you are given the potion of rebirth and relieved of your charms."

"Gammon," Indy said. "I am not sure how I know this, but I need to be Guardian. It is something I feel in my bones."

"Aye, that is what most new heroes usually say. Until they see the Berserker." Gammon said with a sly smile. "Ahhh, I haven't seen a berserker in years though. I like you stranger, I think when you are given a name, even the Valkyrie's will weep with joy."

Indy spoke up without thinking, "I already have a name. It's Indy."

Gammon's mouth dropped open and his arms fell slack to his sides. He sputtered a few times before rushing to Indy's side and clamping a meaty mailed fist over his mouth.

"New heroes don't have names. When the Valkyries choose you, they give you a potion that revives you even from the brink of death. The downside of drink, your memories vanish. Or at least they are supposed to."

"The charms we wear around our necks, they act as a sponge in place of our minds. With so many warriors competing with each other daily, death is a very real aspect of life here. Luckily, it is never permanent. If word gets out you remember your name... well I don't think it will end well for you. There are many jealous men here, men willing to kill you for just looking at them the wrong way. Let alone Odin and the Valkyrie's, I can't imagine what they will do." Gammon dropped his hand from Indy's mouth and pulled him over to a chair.

"Listen, hero. That necklace you wear is everything to you in these halls. If you were to take a mortal wound, you would die, but when the sun rises again you would find yourself lying in that bed over there. The Valkyries see to that. But without your charms, you wouldn't remember anything once again. In simpler terms the charms are your memories... everything you see or learn while you are wearing them is stored within." Gammon said as he motioned at the bed in one corner of the room. The white wood of the bed frame gleamed in the soft light of the room. "Without them, you would have no memory of death. The silver necklace around your neck will create certain charms as you go, each charm will retain specific memories."

"For example," Gammon held up his necklace and pointed to a sword. "This little charm is everything I know about swords. You can see why such a charm is valuable then, right?"

Indy looked at the little charm and nodded slowly, absorbing the strange information.

"So you are saying that if I die, I will lose my memory, but will be revived?" Indy said with worried tone.

"Aye, without your charms, all of your memories will vanish but if you are wearing a charm, you will retain all the memory contained within it."

"Does everyone wear these charms?" Indy asked.

"Only the strangers are free of the memory charms, they are not the men Odin preserves from here to the end of days. They will never know of Ragnarok. There are charms that will aid in your training, charms that will teach you skills and mould you into a fearsome warrior."

"Ragnarok, what is that?" Indy asked.

"Ragnarok... well there are many whispers to what the actual event is. Some call it the end of days, or the final battle. Most agree that when this last fight comes, if we do not win, the world will end, burned in fire and drowned in blood. No one has ever spoken of what foe we will face, but it would have to be a very powerful one indeed."

Indy reflected on Gammon's words, amazed at the dedication needed to maintain the army and the need of its existence. There was no doubt in his mind to the truth of Gammon's words, even without his own memories, just the simple fact of the island floating in the clouds was enough to lend faith to everything. One thing did seem a little puzzling and he aimed his next question at the man before him.

"So how do you remember so much Gammon? You seem like your full of answers and knowledge." Indy said as he eyed the large warrior and necklace full of charms.

Gammon nodded and a large smile creased his face.

"You are a quick one, that is sure." Gammon fingered his necklace that was heavy with multiple charms. "I have secrets beyond these little charms to be sure. If you prove yourself, maybe I might show you some little tricks. To start with, the memory charms themselves are highly prized items in Valhalla. The charms are a form of currency here, they can be traded, sold, stolen or won. On rare occasions a Valkyrie will grant her chosen a gift of one." Gammon looked closer at Indy's charms. "I see you already have an extra charm."

Indy looked down at his necklace and noticed he had two small metal pieces dangling from its silver chain. One was a square disk engraved with a sun, with two swords crossed at the center. The other charm was a small silver feather.

"It appears Kara has chosen a hero after all." Gammon smacked Indy's shoulder with a friendly, but heavy hand. "Kara is one of the newer Valkyries, but she is already one of the most loved. Make her proud young warrior and she will look after you well."

"Let's get you dressed in your armour and I will take you to Odin. You must still prove yourself in battle, it is a tradition that we all must go through on our first day."

Gammon led Indy from the small apartment and into the hallways of the fortress. Indy quickly realized Valhalla was an absolute maze. Hundreds of doors exited the building and long corridors wound their way around the interior of the massive building. Gammon pointed out oversized wooden doors occasionally, each were a smaller subset of buildings named Halls. Each Hall was named something heroic, Halls of the Brave, Halls of the Hero and many, many others.

They passed through a large archway and out onto a wide balcony. From this vantage point, the whole island was exposed below them. Wisps of clouds covered a lush green forest. Several rocky peaks poked through the green curtain of trees and birdcalls sounded out in the distance. Beside him, Gammon paused to prop his elbows on a thick stone railing. He sat there silent and motionless, staring off into the distance. Indy looked in the direction Gammon was staring. The large white tree he had noticed earlier glittered in the distance, its large golden leaves catching the sun as the tree swayed in the breeze. Indy's breath caught in his throat as he admired the splendour of the large tree.

Beside him, he heard Gammon speak.

"The tree of life," he said softly. "Also known as Yggdrasil to some other folk. Beautiful isn't it?"

"Yes, very beautiful, those leaves are... spectacular."

"Aye, they are lad, that they are." Gammon slapped Indy's back and ushered him back on their way.

"Everything outside the walls is off limits," Gammon warned. "Odin has decreed that anyone caught past the walls may forfeit their charms. If they return at all."

"What is that supposed to mean, if they return, I thought even if we die we return to our beds every morning."

Gammon nodded, "True that is, as long as you stay within Valhalla's walls. Outside the walls however, if you die, you will not rise again. Odin will not risk our warriors in senseless combat, no matter the risk or reward. Just remember not to get on Odin's bad side, the man has quite a temper."

"You keep mentioning this Odin guy, who is he exactly?"

"Ah, I keep forgetting you are new here. Odin is the Lord Father and caretaker of Valhalla. A finer warrior you will never meet and wait until you see his wolves, two of the fiercest creatures you will ever lay eyes on. But seeing is believing and we are running late. Let's get moving."

After several more twists and turns through the hallways, Gammon finally led Indy into the Hall of the Heroes. The hall was massive, with a large ring on the floor in the middle of the room. High on the walls were deep alcoves where people had gathered in anticipation of the new hero's battle. The rafters themselves even added to the warrior theme of the room, as they were made of thousands of spears. Hundreds of shields adorned the walls and racks of weapons surrounded the wide ring. In the middle of the ring, a man stood clad in thick dark armour. He had his back to Indy and his head was raised to the large alcove above.

Indy was led into the ring by Gammon, who gave him a few words of encouragement. "Don't worry about dying hero, just do yourself proud in battle." Gammon swatted Indy as he left him and the other warrior standing in the ring.

In the alcove above, men were filing in and taking their seats. At the very center of the group, a large man sat in a massive carved chair. He wore a golden circlet over short blonde hair. A black patch covered one eye and the other blue eye seemed to glow with an eerie haze. The man was enormous, easily dwarfing everyone in the alcove, and there was not an ounce of fat on him. Indy seemed to shrink under the man's hard stare and felt only relief when his blue gaze slid past.

Behind the large man, women wearing white sleeveless dresses entered the alcove carrying large jugs and trays of metal cups. Their white dresses shimmered as they twirled and moved through the audience serving each man until everyone had a full cup.

The large man raised a hand for silence and then his booming voice filled the hall, "Welcome hero! You have been chosen by my Valkyries as a prospective warrior for my army. Prove yourself in battle and you may follow us into the sunset of the world until the last battle rages and my army floods the land below."

The large man, who was obviously Odin, cast his gaze down on the two men in the ring again. Indy shuddered, as the blue eye seemed to see right through him.

"Indeed this is a special day," Odin said, his words echoing around the room. "Kara has chosen an avatar at last!"

Cheering erupted around the room and the men stomped their feet and clapped their hands at the news.

The man beside Indy turned to look sharply at him and muttered, "That charm will be mine little worm."

The man's eyes were dark and his skin even darker. When he smiled at Indy, it looked like even his teeth were blackened. A shudder coursed over Indy as he looked at the man beside him, who had now started foaming at the mouth.

Odin lifted his gaze up from the two warriors to address the rest of the room.

"Normally I would have new heroes prove their worth in basic combat, with their fists. Today however, I choose to see what this new avatar is truly capable of. A champion of the Valkyries must be a capable warrior if he is to survive."

Odin pointed at the man standing beside Indy. "Valeth is an extremely capable warrior, he has spent years in the ring honing his abilities. He has volunteered to be your first opponent. You two warriors will have a few moments to choose a weapon from the racks around the ring. When you are satisfied with your weapon, step back into the middle of the ring and wait for my command to start. I grant you use of this weapon as long as you wish, as a reward to commemorate this historic day. Choose wisely."

Indy was sure that Odin had spoken that last part directly to him. Moving towards the racks, he began to browse the weapons. It would not be an easy choice, there were hundreds of weapons. There were so many swords, spears, nets, daggers, pikes and staves. Indy lifted the first sword he came to, it was a long thin bladed weapon but it didn't feel right in his hand. Looking across the ring his opponent was swinging a large two-handed mace around with wide sweeping strikes. As he was watching the other man, his hand fell on something warm. Indy turned to look down on the weapon. Everything else had been cold and hard to his touch but not this one. Under his hand was a long black spear. Its length was filled with carvings of odd serpents and at each end, a small blade shined in the torch light of the room. Looking back up at the alcove, Indy saw Odin nod almost imperceptibly.

Indy took the weapon from the rack and walked into the center of the ring where the other warrior was waiting. Silence dropped on the room as Odin raised his hand once again.

"Warriors ready!" He shouted.

Indy turned to face Valeth, who had raised the large mace over his shoulder. The spear in his own hand seemed to heat up even more as he readied for battle.

"BEGIN!" Odin shouted.

Indy moved like a snake, it was a natural feeling that moved him, something that seemed to drop over his actions and motions like a new skin. The man before him looked like he was moving in slow motion, Indy could see Valeth's muscles and posture changing even before the two handed chop began to descend. Indy's spear blurred and hit Valeth once and then twice in rapid succession. Valeth fell to one knee and Indy had the blade of the spear against the bare spot that opened at the base of the man's helmet.

"Yield." Indy encouraged softly.

His opponent grunted as he moved, rolling forward and diving away. He came up with the mace held in front of his body, ready for Indy's next attack. Eyeing Indy, Valeth cautiously stepped forward, slowly moving back into range. He would be more cautious now, but it would not help. Indy went on the attack, darting forward and extending the spear in a swift move. The spear struck the man on the breast with a thud. The thick metal breastplate cracked and fell to the ground with a crash. Spinning the spear back and around with a flourish, Indy brought it swinging back at the man's head. Valeth ducked the blow easily but the swing wasn't Indy's real attack. Indy's foot came around in a roundhouse kick following the swinging spear. The armour on Indy's boot connected with the warrior's temple and Valeth was out cold before his body hit the floor.

Cheering erupted from the stands as Indy stood over the fallen warrior. A mob of men rushed out of unseen doors, to drag the downed warrior away. In moments Indy was alone in the ring, his head held high and looking up at Odin.

Odin's hand rose into the air for silence.

"Congratulations hero, you have proven yourself in battle and have earned yourself a spot in my army. In the future such victories will earn you memory charms from the fallen. Tonight, in a celebration of your victory, you will feast with my brothers and enjoy ale poured by the Valkyries themselves."

Indy bowed deeply to Odin and smiled, already looking forward to the feast and the opportunity to speak with Kara again.

Chapter 8 – Valhalla - Warm Wings

The feast was held in a gigantic room that served as Valhalla's dining room. Banners hung from spears in the rafters, golden cups were scattered over every long wooden table and men sat at the tables still wearing choice pieces of their prized armour. At the head of the room, Odin sat upon a throne of spears and shields. The extremely large man wore simple robes with black and gold threading weaved into patterns of ravens. At the foot of his throne, lay two large black wolves. The wolves raised their strange blue eyes to watch Indy as he approached Odin's throne.

Bowing his head Indy said, "Greetings Odin."

Odin nodded at Indy and waved to a pair of black cloaked women waiting in the wings. "Bring our new hero something to drink." Odin commanded.

The women moved to obey, scooping up pitchers and goblets from a side table and bringing them to Indy. When the first woman came closer, he saw that it was not a black cloak she wore, but a feathery set of black wings. The wings rested over her shoulders and trailed behind her as she walked. Dark brown eyes regarded Indy from a pale white face that was hard and angular. When the woman spoke, her soft breathy voice soothed Indy instantly.

"Have a drink young warrior, my name is Freyja, and I am leader of the Valkyries. It appears Odin himself has taken a liking to you." She nodded at the spear strapped to Indy's back. "Odin has blessed your weapon and looked kindly on your first fight."

Indy tried to speak to the beautiful Valkyrie but could only manage to say, "Yes... Freyja."

Indy was just reaching for the offered ale when a commotion brought his attention to a new group of people that had entered the hall. A group of men in camouflaged clothing had entered the room and was making their way toward the throne. At the head of the group was a tall man with salt and peppered grey hair and waxy grey complexion. The grey man held his head high with an air of pride and strength. He had his eyes set firmly on Odin as he led the group of men through the dining hall. Muttering and cursing followed the men's arrival as the crowd sitting at the tables watched them pass. It was obvious to Indy there was some ill will between the two groups. Each of the camouflaged soldiers were armed with... Indy had to think a moment before the word came to his mind... assault rifles.

Freyja nodded once and turned from Indy, returning to the side of Odin's throne with the mug of ale.

"Tapper, so nice of you to join us this fine evening." Odin waved at the men and gestured to the tables. "Your little toy soldiers are welcome to have a taste of ale at our tables."

Tapper stopped a few feet to the side of Indy and glared up at Odin. "My soldiers will not drink your cursed wine. We have no desire to stay in these halls for the rest of eternity."

Odin laughed heartily. "Ah well, that is your choice my little friend. Tell me what brings you to my hall then, if not for the ale."

Tapper looked sideways at Indy and then back at Odin. "You know exactly why I am here. You made me a promise and I am here to collect. You have been putting me off for weeks now and I demand you..."

Thunder filled the hall as Odin stood, rage crossing his face like a thunderstorm. The wolves at his feet stood and bared their long teeth.

"You dare talk to me like that in my own hall!" Odin shouted, a silver spear appearing in his hand out of thin air.

Tapper stood still as a stone, but he did not back down.

"My apologies for my tone Odin, you must forgive me, but I am only thinking of my country men who are threatened by enemies at every turn. I meant no disrespect."

The thunder cleared from the room and Odin sat back down in his throne. The wolves sat back on their haunches but they still watched Tapper with barely concealed menace.

"I see your point," Odin said as a large smile crossed his face.

Indy wasn't sure but he thought Odin's one good eye flicked to him for a moment.

"You are right, it is past time that I offered up a new trial, as I promised I would.

Odin raised his voice to include the whole hall. "In times of great need, in ages past, Valhalla has sent forth warriors into the lands below to act as emissaries. These emissaries were known as Guardians, and as such, they were given gifts to help aid them in completing tasks that required a delicate touch. The Guardians act outside Valhalla's influence, in places where our army may not tread. As a reward for passing a series of trials, a Guardian is awarded one symbolic gift from my hand. Anyone may attempt these trials but there can only be one winner. A word of warning, once you agree to participate, anyone failing the trial is stripped of their charms and given the potion of rebirth."

The audience murmured quietly as Odin finished speaking. Indy looked to Tapper who was smiling in obvious anticipation.

"Tomorrow morning will be the first day of the trials. Anyone wishing to take part in the trials will present themselves to me in the Hall of the Heroes at dawn."

Odin struck the butt of his spear against the floor for emphasis. "There will be no exchanging of charms this evening. You go into the contest as you stand before me now."

Several members of the audience stopped moving as Odin's words fell over them. Many warriors had started haggling for charms at first mention of the trials, but they all left off the trading at Odin's warning.

Odin stood in one swift motion and cast his silver spear at the far wall. The silver missile whistled as it flew. It hit the wall in a crash of thunder and a flash of lightning. When Indy looked back to the throne, Odin was gone.

Tapper and the soldiers marched from the hall in one tightly packed group. Something about Tapper didn't sit right with Indy and he was about to follow him from the hall when a heavy hand thudded onto his shoulder. Indy looked back to see Gammon smiling broadly at him.

"This is a great turn of events! I can't remember the last time we had two Guardians in Valhalla. Exciting times!" Gammon was clearly drunk and swaying on his feet. Every word that came from his mouth was accompanied by spittle or slurring.

"Are you going to take part in the trials Gammon?" Indy asked.

"Naw, the trials aren't for me." Gammon slurred. "The trials are a great risk, only the most decorated warriors would even consider entering the contest. Well, the most decorated and the naive ones as well." Gammon said as his lone eye rolled back into its socket.

"What do you mean, naive? I was thinking about joining." Indy said as he crossed his arms waiting for Gammon's reply.

It took Gammon a few moments of effort to focus his eye on Indy.

"I meant no disrespect little hero. However, you have to realize the consequences of losing the trial, don't you? Anyone who loses, well, they are pretty much dead. Without your charms the potion of rebirth is like a reset button, you start your training again on day one. I have lost many friends this way. When you awaken a new hero, well, you are never quite the same as you were before."

Gammon patted Indy's shoulder and then continued his slurring, "I hope you're not even considering entering, you have much to lose, and it has been years since a new found hero has been given the blessing of a Valkyrie and a weapon blessed by Odin himself. You had better just watch from the alcoves my young friend. You have been chosen for great things, it would be a shame to lose you now. Although it would be interesting to see if your slight memories would persist through a second rebirth."

Just then, Kara appeared, carrying a tray full of large mugs. All eyes in the room turned to watch her cross the floor of the hall and stop beside Indy's table. The large white wings across her back swept out to either side as she performed a low bow to her champion.

"A finely fought battle deserves a fine reward. The golden ale of Valhalla is a blessing to us all and will strengthen and sustain you for all your years."

Kara straightened from her low bow and placed the tray on the table in front of Indy.

"It is a custom of the Valkyries to serve our warriors this ale every evening from here to eternity. It is my pleasure to bring you your first mug. Drink it with pride, hero, and bring honour to the Valkyries."

The sounds around the hall died away as everyone in the room watched Kara lift one of the mugs from the tray and offer it to her champion. Kara's dark chocolate eyes locked onto his and waited for his response.

Indy looked into her eyes and found himself lost in their depths and unable to find any word of thanks. For several heartbeats, he held her eyes before breaking the spell with a lopsided grin. He took the offered mug and raised it high into the air.

"For the Valkyries and for Valhalla!" he shouted.

Cheers erupted from around the hall as the silence lifted and the feast continued.

Indy poured the entire contents of the mug down his throat and slammed the mug down on the table. The golden liquid seared its way into his lungs as the breath was driven from his chest. Instantly he felt alive and emboldened. His words flowed from his mouth without thought.

"I will bring you great honour, my white Valkyrie. Your every wish is my command."

Kara's eyes flashed and her smile ignited a fire inside Indy like none he had ever known.

"My champion, you will be counted among the greatest heroes Valhalla has ever seen. I have seen your face in my dreams and in those dreams, I see you standing in Odin's hall in victory. Join the trials and prove my dreams. Become a Guardian of Valhalla."

Kara grabbed another mug from the tray and raised it to Indy's lips. Indy's mouth opened to accept the golden ale as Kara began to pour. The fire began to spread through his body, making him feel even more alive.

"Every victory shall be in your Honour, my white princess." Indy said.

The golden ale was loosening everything in his body including his tongue. Indy knew if he did not watch himself, he was going to get in way over his head.

Kara's smile enticed him and the ale seemed to make him feel larger than life. The people in the room around them seemed to drift away as another mug was lifted from the tray and brought to his lips.

As Indy drained away the golden ale was followed by Kara's lips pressing against his in a hard kiss. The fire of the ale was magnified by the feeling of her lips against his. Kara broke the kiss and slid one hand across Indy's chin, wiping away some of the ale that had spilled there.

Kara looked across the table at Gammon.

"Gammon, my champion will require some... extra attention. I will be indebted to you if you would see fit to do your best. Our little warrior here will have a long road ahead."

Gammon nodded his head once and the Valkyrie gave him a wide smile. She smiled again at Indy before scooping up the now empty tray and then walking away. Indy followed her with his eyes until she was lost in the crowd.

"Now that's something you don't see every day." Gammon said with a laugh. "I don't know what Kara sees in you little hero, but her blessing is enough for me."

Gammon looked closer at Indy. For a moment the slurring and spittle disappeared. His voice lowered as he spoke into Indy's ear.

"If you do wish to enter the trials, I may have a few things that may be of some help to you. Come to my forge on the 'morrow. I will show you some of my most prized pieces. If the white Valkyrie wants a champion, then a champion I will give her."

"Come on, let's get outta here, we are going to have a big day tomorrow and I will need to get started right away."

Indy's mind was filled with Kara's voice but he nodded at Gammon and stood unsteadily from the table. Together they began to make their way back to his apartment. The entire journey had Gammon talking excitedly about his forge and how hard Indy would have to train. After bidding a babbling Gammon goodbye at his door, Indy stepped into his darkened apartments and stripped from his armour. There was just enough light in the room to be able to make his way to his bed without crashing into the furniture. When he crawled into his bed, he fell instantly asleep, exhausted from his first day in Valhalla.

When Indy woke in the morning, he was not alone. A large white feathered wing covered him from head to toe and a warmth behind him told him he had a visitor in his bed. Indy stayed perfectly still as the Valkyrie behind him snuggled closer in the small bed.

"Good morning Indy," Kara whispered in his ear, seconds before her teeth nipped his earlobe. The soft-feathered wing brushed him as Kara stood from the bed.

"I was waiting for you to wake, but it looked like you were going to sleep the day away." Kara stretched on the tips of her feet and reached for the sky. Her wings swept out to either side and shook gently before wrapping back around her shoulders. "I hope you didn't mind my company last night. I was a little worried about you, I overheard some of Tapper's men talking about you. I don't know what you did to them, but they really don't like you."

Kara smiled softly as Indy watched her from his bed. The light streaming in from the window illuminated her features. It made her seem something more than beautiful. With her wings, it made her an angel.

"You're beautiful." The compliment rolled off Indy's tongue in the absence of a filter.

Kara's smile seemed to glow in response. The feathers of her white wings preened and a healthy pink glow coloured her cheeks.

A savage look crossed her face as she stepped closer and said, "No one will dare to touch you outside the circles now. I have seen to that."

The Valkyrie turned from Indy's surprised look and strolled from the room. He heard a muffled beating of wings that faded away as she left.

Lying back down on his bed Indy reached up to feel the ear Kara had bitten. His ear throbbed with pain and when he looked at his fingers, he saw a small trickle of blood on his fingertips. Through the pain, Indy felt a small underlying stirring of emotion. However, it was gone just as quickly as it came.

Indy was sitting at his table, tracing the carving of his name when Gammon came strolling in.

"Good morning Hero." Gammon said as he entered.

"Morning Gammon," Indy said rising from his chair to greet the armoured warrior. "It looks like you are feeling a bit better today."

"Aye, that I am, and from what I remember we need to get you a little training in. Best place for that is my forge. But tell me, do you still remember your name hero?"

Indy nodded, "Nothing has changed Gammon. I remember my name but little else." Indy shook his head slowly. "But my head is killing me. What was that stuff we drank last night?"

"Ah, the golden ale of Valhalla, I'm not sure what's in it. Only Odin himself knows for sure. But it is a potent mix, liquid courage in a bottle."

Gammon smiled broadly and patted his belly. "Everything a growing hero needs. You can survive on those spirits alone and never want for any other. But enough small talk, let's get on to business. Follow me."

Gammon led Indy out onto the rooftops that made the floor of this level. The fortress was stacked up in levels that slowly built their way up to the top most peak where Odin sat upon his throne. Looking out over the edge, Indy could see a lush forest spreading out for miles on the other side of a solid rock wall. The wall surrounded the fortress and had warriors constantly patrolling its high walkway.

Gammon didn't pause to look out across the island but instead pulled Indy along by the shoulder.

"The fortress has many doors and many more passages, but you will find your way easy enough. My forge is just around the corner on this level."

Gammon led Indy through a series of archways until they found themselves in front of a massive door. On the door was metal emblem of two crossed swords and below that a bed of fire.

Gammon placed one large hand on the door and mouthed a silent word before pushing the door open.

"Here we are lad. Come in and I will give you a little tour."

The forge was a massive round room with a large white box at its center. Racks of weapons and armour filled the walls around the entire room. Large tarps partially covered several chests that were stacked in one part of the room. Each one was covered in thick dust. Gammon led the way to the center of the room and the white box that sat there. On top of the box was a pair of sleek black gloves and a golden feather.

"I haven't had any visitors to my forge in a very long time Indy. Please excuse the mess, I sometimes get a bit carried away with my work."

"Work?" asked Indy.

Gammon nodded with a slight smile, "Where do you think Valhalla gets its weapons little hero? Stand back and I will give you a little demonstration."

Gammon ushered Indy several steps away from the white box before putting on the black gloves. He raised the golden feather to his lips and gave it a quick kiss before tucking it into the belt at his waist.

"The forge is a tricky beast to master, you need a strong will and a solid idea in your head to make it work. The slightest bit of confusion would result in failure. The more specific you are the better. Let's see... we will start with a sword. Everyone needs a good sword."

Gammon closed his one eye and placed his black gloved hands onto the box. For a moment, nothing happened. Then with a small flash of light, the box lit up. Gammon opened his eye and then lifted the lid of the box. He reached in and pulled out a gleaming silver sword. The hilt was wrapped in dark leather and the blade shone like the moon.

"That's amazing Gammon!" Indy shouted as Gammon handed him the sword hilt first.

Indy took the blade up and swung it experimentally. The weapon practically sang in his hand as it cut through the air.

"What else can you make with that forge?" Indy asked. "This sword could use a scabbard."

Gammon nodded and closed the box. "Is there anything in particular you wanted worked into the leather? I can do anything, animals, words... you name it."

Indy thought for a moment before requesting, "A couple white feathers maybe and maybe something silver."

Gammon nodded and closed his eye. He reached for the box and within seconds, the light flashed. When he opened the box, he retrieved a black leather scabbard and a belt made of pure silver. The belt buckle was made of two white feathers that crossed together to lock the belt into place.

"Gammon... that is beautiful. You are a true artist."

The smile on Gammon's face threatened to split his head in half. "Thank you Indy, not many warriors appreciate the effort. Most here just want something deadly and the deadlier the better. No one cares much for art. In the past, I used to make some really nice things, statues, vases but now all I ever make are weapons. No one even notices if I put scrollwork on the blades or eagles on the armour. It's maddening I tell you. I stopped making anything nice, it's just not appreciated anymore."

"So you can make more than weapons and armour with the forge?" Indy asked.

Gammon nodded, the light in the room seemed to catch the ruby in his eye. He pointed over to the crates.

"I have made many things in the past. I have kept the best of them in storage, maybe one day they will be of use."

Gammon stepped a little closer to Indy and lowered his voice.

"I will show you more if you wish, but you must promise to hold your tongue. I do not want word of my work getting out. The last thing I need is some fool hero wandering in here to challenge me for my charms. I could lose everything."

"Your secret is safe with me Gammon." Indy promised.

"Speaking of charms," the one eyed warrior said as he lifted a small silver bone charm from his necklace. With a little bit of fiddling the charm came free of the necklace and Gammon held it out to Indy.

"What is it?" Indy asked.

"It is an old training charm I have had for years. Kara wants you to get accustomed to our ways and methods of fighting sooner rather than later. This little bone will teach you some basic martial arts and fighting techniques. Put it on your chain and I will show you how to access the old memories that are locked away inside it."

Indy did as he was told and attached the silver bone to his necklace. Nothing happened. No surge of memory, no feeling of power or strength or even knowledge flowed through him. He looked at Gammon sideways.

"Relax boy. The charms work with your subconscious. You will never be able to access those charms directly. The memories just seep into your awareness, you know, without actually knowing. Crazy stuff eh?"

Indy looked at Gammon in confusion.

"Bah, it is easier to just show you."

Gammon walked over to a weapons rack and pulled out a bow and quiver of arrows. He handed over the weapons and pointed at an armour dummy at the far end of the room.

"The charm you are wearing favours the bow and arrow. You know how to shoot them now, even if you never lifted a bow in your life."

Indy shook his head in disbelief but notched an arrow to the bow and aimed at the far target. Indy tried to line up the shot but struggled to bend the bow. Gammon smacked him in the head.

"Don't think about it, just do it. Let your sub conscious mind guide your hand."

Indy looked quizzically at the warrior but did as he was told. He emptied his mind of all thoughts except the target. In one smooth motion, he raised the bow, pulled back the string and released. The arrow flew true and sunk into the face of the dummy.

"That is pretty cool Gammon," Indy said in disbelief as he exchanged the bow for his sword and stepped toward another dummy next to the nearby chests.

Just then, a piece of armour fell to the floor. Something small and dark scurried away into the dark recesses of the room. Whatever it was ducked under the tarp of the largest chest. Indy raised his sword and charged off in pursuit of the little shadow.

"No!" Gammon shouted as he shoulder charged past Indy to block his path to the crates.

Gammon was a big man and even though he was unarmed, he made an incredible wall. Indy quickly put away his sword and held out his hands, palms up.

"What the hell is that Gammon?" Indy asked looking around Gammon towards where the shadow had disappeared.

Gammon relaxed visibly when Indy's sword was put away. The big man turned away from Indy and walked over to the crates. He stooped over to scoop up a small figure into his large hands.

"I suppose one more secret shared between us won't matter much," Gammon said as he opened his hands.

Inside the warrior's large hands he held a small pink rabbit. The rabbit sat still as a statue as it looked up at Indy with its dark eyes. Only when the rabbit's ears twitched, did Indy even realize it was alive.

Indy looked from the strange pink rabbit to the massive, scarred, one-eyed warrior and back again. Indy had to try really hard not to laugh at the soft expression that was clouding Gammon's face.

"Ah... sorry," Indy said. "I had no idea it was your pet."

"Pinkeh is no ordinary pet." Gammon said briskly. "She is much more."

Gammon's single eye started to tear up.

"I haven't told anyone this before, but when you told me you could remember your name... well, you are not the first person to remember something from your previous life. Pinkeh was the name one of my daughters."

Gammon stroked the small pink rabbit that was no bigger than Indy's fist.

"I have been here for more years than I care to remember Indy. But in all my years, this one creature has stood by my side. She is the only thing I have left from my old life."

Indy put a hand to Gammon's arm. "Your secret is safe with me Gammon. I swear it."

Gammon nodded and turned to let the rabbit scurry away. No sooner had the rabbit disappeared then a gong started to sound in the distance.

Gammon cleared his throat before saying, "The gongs are calling all applicants to the Hall of the Heroes. If you still wish to enter the trials, we must go now."

Indy nodded firmly and said, "Let's go."

Indy and Gammon found their way to the Hall of the Heroes not long after that. Gammon wished him luck before striding away down the hall. Indy walked into the hall alone. The ring at the center of the room was filled with warriors. Armoured warriors of Valhalla on one side and Tapper's mercenaries on the other. Above the ring, Odin and Tapper stood on one of the balconies overlooking the ring. It looked like Odin was just about to speak as Indy walked into the Hall.

"Ah, Valhalla's newest champion," Odin said in greeting. "I was wondering if you would be joining this little group. Enter the ring and declare your intentions."

Indy did as he was told, stepping into the ring and in between the two groups of men. He wore the armour Gammon had given him, the silver sword at his hip and across his back was the black spear of Odin.

"I wish to be Guardian," Indy said simply and bowed his head towards Odin.

Odin clapped his hands and smiled. "Your challenge is accepted hero. Listen while I explain the rules." Odin's voice rumbled in the air, loud enough everyone could hear him clearly. "There are no rules once you enter the circle. Like in life, you must do whatever it takes to win the day. You may use whatever you have at your disposal to win. Winning means the other contestant is unconscious, dead or unwilling to continue. You will be pitted against each other until the clear victor emerges. The spoils of war are yours to collect from the fallen. Take anything you wish from those you defeat, but you may only take one item per fight. Weapons, armour and other trinkets are also fair game."

"The trials will last for as long as it takes to find a victor, you will remain in your rooms at all times you are outside of the ring. The Valkyries will call on you when it is time for your battle. They will escort you to and from the ring as well."

Tapper whispered something into Odin's ear and a broad smile appeared on Odin's face.

"A challenge fight will kick off the trials of the day. It has come to my attention there is a personal matter that needs to be solved on the field of battle."

Odin's eye swept across the people in the ring and pointed out two men.

"Titus, Tsu, step forward."

The first warrior was from Valhalla. He was a tall red headed man with wild eyes and a curved samurai sword on his back. He was clad in brown leather armour and wore a necklace full of charms. The other person Odin had pointed to was a Chinese man in a solid black outfit. The man in black had no visible weapons but moved with a catlike grace.

The other warriors silently moved from the ring, leaving the two combatants to face each other.

"Begin," Odin said as the ring finally cleared.

The samurai sword flowed from is sheath as the red headed Titus moved. In response, Tsu rolled backwards and brought two weapons from the hidden folds of his robes. In one hand, he held a black pistol and in the other, a coiled chain with a weighted end.

The pistol fired twice at the rushing red head with no apparent effect, it was as if Titus had just blurred out of the way. The samurai sword swung and cut the pistol in half. Rolling and flipping away the black figure started to swing the chain until he hurled away with a snap. The chain wrapped itself around the sword like a snake. From out of another pocket, Tsu produced a handful of sparkling dust. He threw the dust into the air as he danced around the sweeping sword. A second chain appeared in his other hand as the Valhalla warrior stumbled away from the choking dust. Titus coughed and sputtered in the cloud of dust, finally raising a hand from his sword to wipe the dust from his eyes.

Tsu gave a hard tug on the chain and the samurai sword came free for the warrior's grip, clattering to the floor.

Tsu started spinning the chains in his hands again, creating a buzzing noise. He moved his hands in a dazzling pattern that made the man in black hard to see in the torch light. The red headed Titus regained his footing and charged back in, looking to close the distance. The chains struck like hornets. Before he could close the distance, Titus was hit with several stinging blows. Only the leather armour the man wore saved him for serious damage.

The black cladded Tsu spun away, wheeling the chains around him and then coming back in to attack with amazing speed. One chain wrapped around the warrior's leg and the other around his neck. As the first chain was pulled tight, it brought the big man to the ground. But as Titus was falling, Tsu spun around and the other chain was tugged in the opposite direction. The resulting snap echoed in the ring, and only the heavy thud of the body could be heard as it hit the floor.

"Winner, Tsu." Odin said with a hint of approval. "The rest of you return to your rooms. A Valkyrie will call on you shortly."

Indy watched as Tsu stood over the fallen warrior and claimed his prize. Tsu picked up the samurai sword and when he noticed Indy watching, pointed it his way. Indy stared back at Tsu, not backing down in the least as several Valkyries ushered them back to their rooms.

Chapter 9 – Valhalla - Kara's Dragon

Indy waited for the knock on his door announcing his time to fight but it never came. After the first hour of waiting, he grew restless. By the second, he was bored. After that, the time simply faded away along with the sunlight coming through his window. Indy finally decided that no one was coming for him and stripped off the armour and weapons he was wearing. That was when the knock on his door sounded. Perturbed he threw open the door to find a white cloaked Kara. Without a word, she stepped in the room and into his arms. Her head landed softly on his shoulder as she began to weep. Indy cradled her in his arms and closed the door behind her.

"What's wrong Kara?" He asked into her dark hair. Kara didn't answer but continued to cry quietly. Indy held her close until the Valkyrie was finally able to speak.

"These trials are... difficult for me. I feel connected to each warrior and to make matters worse Odin has forbidden me to be at your side. That evil little grey man has convinced Odin that it was an unfair advantage to have a Valkyrie at your side. I am not even allowed to watch you fight."

Kara broke down again. This time the tears flowed freely and something within Indy changed as well. His eyes started to tear as well. The feeling of helplessness washed over him as he held Kara even closer. Indy murmured to her that it would be okay, everything would be okay. More emotions started to batter him. His heart started to ache with desire, and a heartbeat later, he found Kara's lips pressing against his in a savage yet passionate kiss.

"They will kill you if you are not ready my champion." Kara said between kisses. "I don't know why they hate you so, but the grey man wishes for your blood. I have heard him order your death every day you have been here."

"The grey man?" Indy asked. "You mean Colonel Tapper?"

Kara nodded as she broke away from his embrace. "They will come for you in the night and I won't be able to stay by your side. I must leave soon."

Kara's eyes flashed as Indy felt another emotion sweep through him. Before he knew it, Kara had him by the hand, dragging him through the door and out into the night.

A ring of men were waiting for him just outside the door. Each wore black cloaks with hoods covering their heads, hiding their faces in shadow. The men were startled as the door burst open and Indy and Kara rushed out. However, their surprise was only momentary and an instant later, their weapons came out. Indy recognized three of the faces in the crowd in a sudden moment of clarity. He wasn't sure where he had seen them before but in his mind, he remembered seeing them swarm through a doorway in a bunch. The first man through the door raised a gun and then a flash...

Kara wrapped Indy in her arms as a tearing noise filled the air and the thin tendril of memory was broken. Pieces of shredded white cloak exploded away from Kara's white wings as they unfurled and beat the air. Indy was lifted clear off the ground and rocketed up into the night sky, leaving a very angry group of men in their wake.

Kara raced through the sky and out over the wall. The forest below rushed by in a blur until they came to rest at a small silver lake. The white Valkyrie set him down easily and released her hold on him. Without a word, she rushed from his side and dove under the silver water. A flash of light followed her splash and a heartbeat later, a large swan bobbed to the surface. The swan swam away from him and into the center of the pond where several other swans had already gathered.

Indy dropped to his knees at the side of the pond and watched the swans in a peaceful silence.

"Kara?" he called out into the night.

Indy watched the swans swim for several minutes before the sounds of the forest started to echo around him. With a start, Indy realized he was in trouble. He was alone and unarmed in a strange place. Gammon had warned him of the forest, but he hadn't been very specific about its dangers. Indy listened to the sounds of the woods around him. He could hear birds, maybe monkeys and after a few moments... something larger.

Whatever it was, it was coming closer. Looking around Indy had few options. He could go into the water, stay where he was, or... he looked at a thick Willow tree that was hanging over the edge of the pond. He settled on the tree, it would provide him with excellent cover. With any luck, he would be well hidden if nothing else.

The tree was a breeze to climb and he scurried up as high as the branches would let him. Indy remained silent as something big entered the area around the pond. The leaves of the willow tree were all at once a blessing and a curse. Whatever was out there couldn't see him but at the same time, Indy couldn't see it either. Something huffed near the tree several times and then went silent. A few minutes after that, whatever had been down there crashed back into the forest and away from the pond.

Indy breathed a deep sigh of relief but decided it would be safer to stay put for the night. He wedged himself into the V of the tree and closed his eyes.

A sense of love filled him as he slept and for an instant, he thought he heard a soft female voice. "Kara stop that, you need to control your emotions or you will ruin the boy."

Another female voice answered, "I can't help it, he is just so adorable."

"You must try child. If what Odin says in true, this one must survive."

Indy smiled at the soft voices but couldn't find the strength to open his eyes. A sense of weightlessness filled him and he dreamed he was flying.

A soft warm weight covered his body and when Indy finally woke, he found that again, he was covered by a large white wing.

Behind him Kara spoke, "Morning Hero."

The feathered wing lifted from his body and Kara stood from the bed.

"That was quite the night wasn't it? I am sorry I brought you into the forest but I had no choice. Those men would have killed you last night."

Indy nodded, not doubting for a second that against that many men, he really had no chance.

"Thank you Kara, but what happened to you? One second you are diving into the water, the next, a white swan pops up where you should have been."

"The pond is our little oasis, a safe place for the white Valkyries to roost when we revert to our other form, the swan. The change happens almost every night and while we are changed, we are vulnerable. The silver water is our only safe haven, nothing may enter its waters except for one of us."

"I didn't realize you could change your form, that's cool. I mean, I knew you were different with the whole wings and everything."

"Valkyries are the servants of Odin, each one of us is chosen in the heartbeats before our death. My fellow Valkyries saved my life and in return, I was to choose to follow the way of the raven or the swan. The ravens are Valhalla's spear sisters, born for battle, while the swans are Valhalla's shield maidens, tasked to save the lives of warriors about to die on the battlefield. The heroes we save fill the Halls of Valhalla until the final battle."

"So you are saying I died?" Indy asked.

"Well, not exactly," Kara said slyly. "I watched your battle from above. When you were defeated and tossed into the ocean... well I did not want you to die. Something moved me to save you before you actually died. Please don't tell anyone else that, we are supposed to wait til the fallen have breathed their last breath. I just couldn't let that happen, you were so amazing, standing against Valhalla's Guardian and his goons."

"I was amazing?" Indy blushed with pride.

Kara nodded and ducked her head. "If it wasn't for the interference of another one of Eden's warriors, you would have had a chance at a glorious death, instead of drowning in the water."

Kara turned to face the door of the room. "The trials are starting hero. The Valkyries are being summoned to Odin's hall. Fight well."

Kara kissed him on the lips and turned for the door. "I will see you soon," she said as she disappeared through the door.

Indy watched her go and then began to pace his room as he waited for his turn in the ring. He was expecting Kara as his escort but when a black clad Freyja walked in the room, he hid his disappointment well.

"Hello Freyja," Indy said with a lopsided grin.

"Hello Hero," Freyja said with a breathy voice.

Walking into the room, she seemed to be larger than life and almost bulled Indy into a corner with her presence alone. Her fine black robes wrapped tightly around her well-muscled body. The large black wings that were raised slightly off her shoulders only added to her presence. Indy tried to back away as Freyja stepped closer but he was held in place by the wall at his back.

"A little bird told me of your story. I am told you were the greatest warrior of the little beach skirmish."

Freyja had leaned toward him, bringing her mouth ever closer to Indy. He could feel her breath on his face as she spoke. The smell of black liquorice seemed to fill his nose as her long black hair fell across his shoulder. Her eyes locked onto his as she grabbed him by the hair and turned his head to the side. A dark look passed over her face as she noticed Kara's bite mark upon his ear lobe.

"I see that you have already had a Valkyrie claim you... that is... unfortunate." Freyja held her position a moment longer, before stepping away. "Come hero, it is time, bring your weapons."

Freyja watched as Indy prepared and when he was ready, took him by the hand. She led him down the silent halls until they reached the Hall of Heroes.

"Good luck, your opponent is a favourite among the warriors. His name is Janis." Freyja ushered him into the door without following and it closed behind him with a solid bang.

Indy walked to the ring where Janis was already waiting. The man was a giant, like many of the other heroes of Valhalla. He wore shining blue armour that was layered like the scales of a fish and his weapon was a large black battle-axe. The head of the axe was so massive it could easily double as a shield. Janis watched him enter the ring and gave a slight nod of his head before turning to stare up into the alcove above. Indy lifted his head and waited for Odin's signal to begin.

"Begin," Odin commanded without any fanfare.

Janis was the first to swing and like before time seemed to slow around them. Indy brought his spear up to pick the swinging axe out of the air, but Indy was not prepared for the strength behind that swing. Although the blade looked like it was barely moving, it was only Indy's perception that slowed the swing. The spear was torn from Indy's hand and spun across the floor, out of reach.

Instantly time began to flow like normal if not faster. The only saving grace for Indy was that with such a great swing and heavy weapon, Janis took a long time to recover from the effort. Indy was able to step into his opponent with a series of heavy blows to the man's side before he was forced to backpedal when he was threatened by the large axe.

From there it was a game of diving and rolling. Janis was more careful after the first heavy blow and the large axe rarely buried itself in the floor. Indy's only chance was to retrieve the spear. Janis knew that and kept Indy away from the fallen weapon. At this rate, it was only a matter of time before the axe found its mark and they both knew it. Indy decided he had to take a chance and trust in his armour. If his plan didn't work it would be the end, but without his spear, it would be the end anyway. Indy ducked and rolled until he was in the perfect spot. His chance came on Janis's backhand swing. Indy just barely ducked out of the way of a hard strike, leaving his back wide open. Janis took the shot, even though the man was off balance. The blow shattered Indy's spinal guard and knocked him down to the ground in a long slide. Pain blossomed through every inch of his body, but that pain was quickly drowned out when Indy's hand grasp the spear. Janis's blow had caused Indy to land atop the fallen spear.

Time slowed again as Indy held the spear and for an instant, Indy saw a look of fear slowly crossed Janis's face. This time, Indy didn't wait for the heavy axe to fall. The spear became a blur in his hands, twirling and spinning, it crashed down into the scaled blue armour several times before Janis could react. Indy continued to duck and dodge the slow moving axe. The spear stuck Janis after his every swing, cracking several pieces of armour and causing them to fall to the floor, useless. As the fight wore on Janis began to understand his folly. Indy was taking him apart piece by armoured piece. When the last of his armour hit the floor, Janis sunk to his knees in surrender.

"Mercy," Janis said quietly.

Indy stood behind the man holding the spear's tip to the base of his head, not sure if it was a ploy or not. Looking up to the alcove, Indy looked for Odin's response. Odin looked back with his one eye, waiting to see what Indy would do.

Indy had no desire to kill this man, so he stepped back from Janis and planted his spear in the floor.

Janis looked back over his shoulder and nodded at Indy. "Thank you hero, you fought well, please take this as your victory reward." The warrior took a small object from his necklace. "It is... very special, a great prize."

Tossing it to Indy, Janis walked from the ring. Indy caught the charm and watched Janis leave the room, head held high. Only when he was gone did Indy open his palm to see what Janis had given him. It was a small silver cube.

Chapter 10 – Valhalla - White Tree at Midnight

Both Kara and Gammon were waiting in his apartment to congratulate Indy. Gammon slapped him hard on the back and led him to the small table at the center of the room. On the table was a large pitcher of golden ale and two silver mugs.

"Kara has brought us some ale, drink up and we shall celebrate your first of many victories!"

The white Valkyrie smiled at him and began to pour the golden liquid into their cups. They knocked their mugs together and downed the sweet golden ale. Tingling filled his body as the liquid started to burn its way down into his core. Instantly Indy was revitalized and felt as if he had eaten an entire meal.

Gammon leaned forward and held out his hand. "Now let's see this charm that Janis has given you. I have heard from others that his cube was a source of great knowledge, even if Janis hadn't ever been able to activate it."

Indy held out the small silver cube and Gammon plucked it off his open palm. Gammon studied the little charm closely and then did something that Indy didn't expect. He closed his one good eye and held the little cube in front of his red gem eye.

"Ahhh, I can see great power in this little beauty. It reminds me of the feather in my forge. It has the same kind of power radiating from it... old power, the kind I can't make."

"Hang on a sec...." Indy looked closer at the red gem stuck into Gammon's eye socket. "You can see with that gem?"

Gammon nodded once but remained fixated on the silver cube.

"I don't have a clue what the cube can do though. It could be anything, it doesn't activate when held, and there is nothing to manipulate on its surface..." Gammon considered the cube with a growing curiosity. "I could run a few tests on it, but at a guess, it is a keystone."

"What's that mean?" Indy asked.

"A keystone is an artifact that activates or controls another artifact. Much like the golden feather activates my forge. The real question will be what is this a key too?"

Indy shrugged. "Janis just said it was important, one of his most prized objects, but he didn't say anything else."

Gammon handed the cube back and Indy placed it onto his charm necklace.

Kara wrapped one wing protectively around Indy and eyed Gammon. "Gammon, you have been a great friend to us and I need to ask you a favour. My champion has become the target of Tapper's little henchmen. During the day, I will be able to protect him, but at night... well... he needs a place to stay that is a little more secure."

Gammon looked at the wing wrapped around Indy and whistled softly. He leaned back in his chair and studied the pair a little closer.

"Well that explains a lot. I wasn't sure if it was the ale or not but I thought... You have bonded him then?"

Kara nodded and held her head high.

"Does Odin know? Did he give you permission?" Gammon demanded.

Kara's defiant look seemed to slip and that was enough of an answer for Gammon.

"Pftt... If Odin finds out, he will not be happy. You were told the rules Kara, Odin must approve of all unions, especially when a Valkyrie is involved."

"Hang on a second. What are you talking about Gammon? Bonded? Union?" Indy looked up at Kara and felt a wave of emotion rush over him.

Love, lust, passion and a little tinge of regret flooded over him all at once. The power of the emotions rocked him back into the soft white wing.

"I couldn't help it Gammon," Kara said defensively. "Something happened when I rescued him in Eden. It was as if I had been caught by a trap. I couldn't help myself, I tried leaving him, I really did. Even when I left him in this room, I felt an urge to return and watch over him. The farther away he was, the more I felt the need to return to his side. I can't explain it any more than that."

Gammon eyed the white Valkyrie and nodded.

"It is not the first time a Valkyrie has acted this way. I have heard tales of other Valkyries becoming enthralled with their champions but you must bring this to Odin's attention. Sooner rather than later." Gammon nodded once with finality.

"I will. I promise. But until then I still need your word you will watch him and shelter him the nights when I cannot."

"Aye, bring him to the forge tonight, I will see him safely through the night."

Indy looked from Gammon to Kara and back again. All of a sudden, he felt life in Valhalla just got a lot more complicated.

Indy walked into the forge later that night to find Gammon waiting for him.

"Indy, come over here, I want to see that cube of yours. Since we are going to be locked away for the night, I thought we might be able to work on that puzzling little cube."

Indy slipped the little charm from his necklace and handed it over to Gammon. Holding the cube up to the light Gammon inspected it then walked over to his forge. He slipped the black gloves over his hands before placing the cube beside the golden feather and began to mutter as he compared the two artifacts.

"Aye, their signatures are almost exactly the same. It has to be a key of some sort, the power levels are fairly constant too, no real fluctuations."

Gammon continued to mutter as he brought forth a tool belt from behind the forge and started poking and prodding the cube with various small tools.

Indy left the man to tinker and started to walk around the room. The weapon racks were his first stop but after swinging a few of the weapons around, he moved on. The armour rack was next and he searched through some fantastic items. All of the armour had a sense of real artistic flare, most of the pieces on display had images engraved or sculpted onto their surface. A rustling noise near the covered chest got Indy's attention. He walked over to the tarps to find a little pink rabbit watching him from shadows.

"Hello Pinkeh," Indy said as he reached out a tentative hand.

The rabbit didn't even twitch as he brought his hand down to touch it's soft pink fur. Indy could feel the animal's heartbeat racing as he stroked it.

"That's a good bunny, I'm not going to hurt you little guy."

The little rabbit relaxed slightly but zipped away when Indy looked back to Gammon. Indy smiled at the retreating rabbit and walked back to the forge. Gammon was still muttering at the little cube, obviously, he had not gotten any further in finding out its purpose.

A sense of fear passed through Indy a second before a phantom pain sprang up in his arm. A burning ache formed in his arm and Indy realized at the same moment, something was wrong. Without thinking, he turned and ran to the door. Gammon reached him as he was trying to wrench the large wooden door open.

"Whoa now Indy, where are ya going?" Gammon asked as he spun Indy around to look at his face.

Indy's face was pale his eyes glossy as he spoke. "Kara's hurt Gammon... I don't know how I know, the bond I guess. I have to go to her, she needs me."

"That is not a good idea Indy, Kara should be in the pond right now. If she isn't, then this might be a trap. Someone has unwisely imprisoned her. When Odin finds out, there will be consequences. Just stay here and I will send word to Odin, he will deal with it himself."

Pain blossomed in Indy's chest this time, dropping him to the floor.

"There is no time Gammon." Indy pointed to the north, "I can sense her there."

"Okay, okay, just give me a second. You won't be able to pass the wall without help though."

Gammon ran back to his forge and picked up the little golden feather. He closed his eye in concentration and put his gloved hands to the forge. After the forge flashed with light, he raised the lid to pluck out a small white ball. Again, his hands went to the box and it flashed again. This time Gammon pulled out a small platform with several long handles and dials.

"Quickly Indy, that archway there leads to the forges roof. Take this ball and I will grab the catapult."

They ran through the archway and up a short flight of stairs before bursting out into the open air.

"Okay step on the platform and point to where you sense your friend." Gammon instructed as he setup the device.

Indy did as he was told and pointed towards a section of the forest outside of Valhalla's wall.

"She's there, hurry Gammon."

As he stepped onto the platform, it started to glow blue and Indy felt his feet adhere to its surface.

Gammon nodded as he pulled several levers. The platform Indy was on swung around and tilted to the side, bringing him in line with the direction he had pointed to.

"Once you are over the wall break the orb onto your chest. The ball it forms will absorb the impact and then break apart once you are on the ground. I warn you though, if you drop that little ball or fail to break it on your chest, you will not survive this landing."

Indy nodded.

"Thank you Gammon."

"Good luck Indy." Gammon said as he pulled the largest of the levers.

The air streaked by as the platform launched Indy up into the sky. The wall and then the forest below was a blur as Indy was thrown high into the night sky. Indy clutched the small white ball tightly in his hand and then smashed it into his chest. The air around him shimmered and then frosted. A thick gel wrapped itself around his body and then started to expand. The gel kept expanding until it formed a large ball that was an exact copy of the one he had just been holding. As the large gel ball arced through the air, it began to spin. Indy lost sight of the ground as the ball spun him around. Seconds later, it crashed into the forest below. The gel around him shattered like glass and left him on the ground face down in a pile of powder.

Indy lifted his head to gauge his surroundings. He was near the silvery pond, on the edge of the forest and close to the willow tree he had used as a hiding spot the previous night.

There was no one in sight. Three white swans drifted around the center of the silvery pond but none of them looked spooked or injured. Indy shifted his attention into the woods around the pond and listened. The woods were quiet, nothing moved in the darkness. At the edge of the pond, there was a rustling in the reeds. Floundering in the water was a large swan with a bloody wing. As Indy watched, the swan fought its way through the reeds and out into the center of the pond. Somewhere behind him a branch broke, without thinking Indy dove to the side and a large shape flashed by. In a blink, several men rose from the reeds at the edge of the water.

"It's about time you showed up. We were just about to give up on you and have a little... dinner," one of the shadows said.

Another one of the shadows spoke, his voice harsh. "It's time for a little payback Locke. You might have gotten the jump on us last time but now that your little dragon tattoo is gone..." The man smiled wickedly and pulled out a long knife.

"He is mine Hatch, put away that little tooth pick of yours." The largest of the men said as he walked into the moonlight.

Indy recognized him, it was the man from his flashback. He had been the first man through that doorway, the one with the gun. Indy struggled to remember more but after the gun went off, his mind was a blank.

"Damn it Rick, the kid doesn't even remember you. Let's just check him for that piece of metal Tapper wants and get the hell outta here. This place is spooking me something fierce."

"Suck it up Matt, this will only take a sec. Zeus would have wanted it this way." Rick said advancing on Indy.

Indy was outnumbered and cornered. Running wasn't an option so he drew his only weapon and waited for the men to come at him. The silver sword flashed in the pale moonlight as Indy held it in front of him. He recognized the men now, they were the same ones that were outside his door the previous night. Only Tsu was not with them this time. Four against one, it would be hard, but he had no choice.

The men stopped their advance as a growl issued from the woods to their right. A large blue shape rose from the darkness and started to move through the trees toward them. Whatever it was, it was large, maybe ten to twelve feet high and almost as wide. The men around Indy hesitated as the creature started to rush at them. More growls came from the woods all around them. They were surrounded on all sides, shapes were moving in from the darkness and the men started to panic.

Matt lifted an assault rifle to his shoulder and started to fire at the approaching shapes. The dark blue creature rushed into the clearing and launched the man into the silvery water with a heavy punch. Before the mercenary landed in the water, a buzzing noise filled the air and his motion was halted in midair. He hung there motionless for an instant before he was hurled away into the woods like a ragdoll.

Indy turned from the chaos of the attack and ran for the woods. Gunfire filled the night behind him as he ran. Other things were crashing in the woods around him as Indy ran. The noise of the assault rifles filled the air and several of the bullets buzzed through the woods behind him. Whatever was in the woods around him ignored his flight and moved in the direction of the gunfire.

The path Indy took wasn't very wide but it was the clearest path he saw and right now, all he wanted to do was get away from the men and the beasts behind him. A howling noise filled the air as something else caught his scent and crashed after him in pursuit. Indy continued to run, not knowing where he was heading but knowing that he needed to find some cover or a least a defensible position. The path he was on led further away from the fortress walls but he did remember one place he might be able to make a stand.

At the end of the path he was on was the white tree. In the dark, the white wood of the tree was like a pale ghost in the night. It was the tallest of the trees around but as Indy reached its thick trunk, he found that it had easy handholds. With a great leap, he grabbed the lowest thick branch and heaved himself into the shadowy branches.

Up he went, moving as fast as he could. The howling was getting closer and soon two wolves burst out of the forest and flowed across the ground to the base of the tree. The two great wolves were Odin's, Indy recognized the dark black fur and blue eyes instantly. The wolves circled the tree and lifted their gaze up into the shadowy branches. Indy hid in the thick branches but he knew that the wolves could either see him or smell him.

A horn sounded in the distance, its mournful sound echoed through the forest. The wolves lifted their heads to the sound and bayed a long howl in response. The wolves gave one last longing look at the white tree and then raced off into the night.

Indy's heart threatened to beat itself out of his chest as he watched the two wolves leave. It was a struggle to catch his breath but for the moment, at least he was safe.

He hoped that the wounded swan would recover, but Indy had no sense of the Valkyrie through his bond with her. Indy settled down to watch the path for any pursuit and waited for Kara to come for him.

Unfortunately, the Valkyrie that came for him was not Kara. As the sun rose high is the east, the black winged Freyja landed beside him on the thick white branch.

"You have had a busy night hero. It is not wise to travel these woods in daylight, let alone in the dark of night. But you did manage to find the safest spot in these woods." Freya nodded into the higher branches where several other dark winged Valkyries perched. "My sisters and I enjoyed your company last night. It has been ages since we have had company in our home."

Freyja's wide smile made Indy a little uneasy but he gave her his best lopsided grin.

"I didn't mean to intrude Freyja, a pair of wolves were looking for a little midnight snack so I climbed the tree to avoid them."

Freyja returned the lopsided grin with one of her own.

"Oh little hero, Kara has chosen a very unique avatar and to tell you the truth I am quite jealous. There is something about you I find... very interesting. Very interesting indeed, if you ever find yourself in need of... anything, just call on me. A trustworthy friend is hard to come by in Valhalla."

Freyja looked toward the towering fortress of Valhalla in the distance.

"It seems the trials are about to start, shall I be your escort today, my friend?" Freyja asked in her breathy voice.

Indy looked to the Valkyries watching from above and back to Freyja.

"I would love for you to be my escort today, thank you." Indy said.

Freyja took wing from her perch, beating her wings hard to hover in front of his branch. She spread her arms wide and motioned for him to jump to her. Indy looked to the distant ground and back to Freyja's waiting arms.

"I will catch you, have faith hero." Freyja said, as the grin on her face grew wider.

Indy didn't have much choice, he didn't want to spurn his only way back into Valhalla. Kara would have been here by now if she had been able. Indy looked into the forest in the ponds direction before taking a deep breath and jumping from the branch.

Chapter 11 – Valhalla / Eden - Drop Shipping

Indy was escorted by Freyja to the doors of the Hall of the Heroes. She paused beside him and gave him a lingering kiss on the cheek.

"You have proved yourself a capable warrior. My sister is lucky to have you as her avatar. No matter how your next fight ends, I count myself blessed you have come into our lives."

The leader of the Valkyries smiled a familiar lopsided grin at him and stepped away. She spoke with a pair of Valkyries that were guarding the door to the hall. Indy couldn't hear their hushed conversation but watched the anger build on Freyja's face.

"It seems that a bit of foul play has occurred during the course of the night. Several contestants have dropped or removed from the lists, including some mercenaries that were found in the woods near the white Valkyries roost."

Freyja's voice dropped to a soft whisper, "It seems that someone got the better of four of them last night. Odin has already offered those mercenaries up to the heavens for safekeeping.

After all of this disruption, it looks like there is only one duel left to determine the winner of this trial... yours."

Freyja looked Indy up and down as another Valkyrie came striding in from a rooftop archway. The Valkyrie handed a large sack to Freyja along with a long black spear.

"Here are your weapons, bring honour to the Valkyries young warrior." Freyja said, handing Indy his gear and watching as he equipped himself. "Your last opponent in the trials is Tsu. He will be a difficult adversary, he is a very skilled warrior with many tricks to compliment his natural skill. Be patient and don't fall for his tricks, trust in yourself and you will do well. Good luck."

Indy nodded and touched Freyja's black wing. "Thank you Freyja, you have been a good friend. Tell Kara... well tell her..."

"You can tell her yourself, when you are done with this contest." Freyja said with a nod. "She survived the attack in the woods and is recovering in the ponds healing waters. Now prepare for your battle... it is time."

The doors of the Hall opened and Indy walked into the hall for the last battle. Many other warriors were waiting in the alcoves above while Odin watched Indy enter from his large throne. At the center of the ring, Tsu waited for him. The man was wearing the same outfit he had been wearing the first day of the trial, the only difference Indy could see was the samurai sword sheathed across his back. Tsu ignored his approach and raised his head to look toward Odin, awaiting the command to begin.

Indy stepped into the circle and nodded at Odin. The large one-eyed warrior scowled down at him with a fiery blue gaze. A sense of foreboding filled Indy as Odin's gaze rooted him to the spot. Something was wrong. Indy could sense a change in the room as if the temperature had dropped several degrees.

Odin rose from his throne and raised his voice so all could here. "This is the final duel of the Trial of the Guardian. The winner will become Valhalla's newest Guardian. The loser will embrace death. Odin's blue gaze fell across the two combatants, freezing them both in place. Indy felt himself shrink away from the gaze although not a muscle in his body twitched.

"You both are very capable warriors, champions in every right. I despair losing either one of you to this contest but that is the way of the world. True choices are few and far between. Prepare now my sons. Death or glory awaits."

Indy readied his weapon and slowed his breathing. The spear in his hand felt warm and solid. Tsu stood across from him, his sword bared and pointed at Indy's heart.

Odin bellowed his command, "Begin!"

Time flowed... like normal. Tsu weaved his blade with easy grace at a speed Indy's eyes could hardly follow. The blade spun and then flowed into a strike. Indy stepped back from the swing, without engaging weapons and Tsu stepped quickly back out of range of the longer spear. They began to circle each other, swinging occasionally, trying to feel each other out. Hoping to detect a weakness in the other's defense. Tsu drifted close enough for Indy to nudge him with his spear. Indy spun the spear and hopped away as Tsu chopped at where his feet had been only seconds ago.

"Tricky," murmured Indy.

Tsu smiled as he backed out of range. From inside his black cloak he pulled a small dagger. Indy recognized the problem instantly, with a small blade like that Tsu had changed the dynamics of the fight. Indy now had to contend with a throwable weapon as well as a blade that may have powers that would aid Tsu in his fight. Instead of waiting on Tsu to act, Indy took the offensive. The spear twirled in a fast spiral pattern before shooting straight out at Tsu. The Chinese man dropped below the blade and rolled at Indy's legs. The collision sent Indy sprawling.

Several fast knife attacks rained off Indy's armour as he struggled to regain his feet. Pieces of armour clattered to the floor as Indy spun away and swept the spear in front of him. The spear sliced the black cloak of Tsu nearly in two. A large rent appeared in his chest as black rings of metal fell to the floor like rain drops.

The smile disappeared from Tsu's face and he backpedalled to gain some distance on the sweeping spear. Both men were breathing hard now as they began circling again. Indy needed to press his advantage, so he started swinging the spear in wide arcs. A lucky strike knocked the samurai sword to one side and Indy flowed into Tsu with a long flipping kick. His foot connected solidly with Tsu and sent the man sprawling to the ground, both the sword and dagger bouncing from his grasp. Indy wasn't going to take any chances granting mercy, he had seen Tsu's form of mercy given to others. As Indy prepared to strike, a small metal cylinder rolled to his feet. For a strange instant, Indy thought he knew what the cylinder was.

"Flash ba..."

Light exploded and thunder rang in his ears. Indy dropped to the floor stunned.

When Indy awoke from the blackness, he felt a soft feathery wing covering his body. He knew that the warmth at his back was Kara even before her sweet voice whispered in his ear.

"My hero, I am so sorry for you," Kara said, hugging him closer.

Indy was sure he could hear her crying softly in the darkness of the room, "I will miss you Indy. I wish I could convince Odin to make an exception but he has refused to even see me."

"What happened?" Indy asked. "Are you okay? The last thing I remember was a bright light."

Kara lifted her head to look in his eyes. Her dark brown eyes look tired and red.

"I will survive, thanks to you Hero. The pond healed my wounds after a time, but we have other things to discuss, things far more important than my worries."

Kara hugged him one more time before continuing. "Tsu had one last trick up his sleeve, a trinket from the world below. When you fell, he claimed victory. He also claimed Odin's staff as a spoil of war. From what the other Valkyries are saying, Odin is beside himself with rage.

There is nothing he can do about it though. Deception is part of war. In his eyes, Tsu might not have been the better fighter, but he was the winner of that battle. At the end of the fight, Tsu declared that your death is his only wish as reward for winning the trials. He would have claimed your life at that very instant, if Odin had not interceded. Odin wishes to honour you with a warrior's true death, not a cold blooded murder."

"I will have to remember to thank Odin." Indy smiled and tried to relax. "It was a good fight, I am not ashamed of losing." Indy said as he closed his eyes again. "When am I to take the potion?"

"You will not become one of the reborn, like the others, you will not rise again from this death my love." Kara said softly.

Kara rose from the bed and walked to the door. "We come for you at dawn. Goodbye my Indy." Kara left him in the dark and Indy listened as her wings took her away.

Indy lay in bed staring up at the dark ceiling and watching the shadows dance from a flickering candle on the table. He had several options and paths he could follow. He knew that if he asked Gammon, he could use the catapult again. He might even be able to slip through the wall past the guards unaided. But what would he do after that? The forest was full of strange creatures and prowling wolves. Even if he could survive those for a time, there was still the fact he was on a floating island. No, there was really no choice after all.

At dawn, they came for him. Horns blew to announce the approach of the Valkyries. Indy walked to the door and stepped outside. To his dismay, thousands of warriors lined the rooftops and windows around him. A cheer went up when the crowd spotted him exit the building. Indy's heart surged with pride as he looked around the walls of Valhalla. Gammon separated himself from the crowd and walked to Indy's side.

"Indy," Gammon said with evident emotion. "You have been a great friend and an honourable warrior. You will be sorely missed."

Gammon's heavy hand landed on his shoulder and pulled Indy into a fierce hug. "The Valkyries will carry you to heaven on their shields. May the next world be as good to you as this one. Farewell friend."

Three Valkyries landed before them and walked towards Indy. Kara, Freyja and Lana bowed to him and placed three small golden shields on the ground.

Freyja said, "Only in death do we find our true master."

"Only in death do we find true peace," Kara said.

"Only in death do we follow our last path," Lana said.

"Lie down on the shields hero, let us bare you into the next world with honour." Freyja commanded.

Indy did as he was told and settled down on the smooth golden shields. When he was finally still the three Valkyries knelt down and lifted Indy and the shields from the ground. With a burst of air, the Valkyries rose from the ground, carrying Indy between them. They rose slowly at first, giving the crowd one last glimpse of him. Soon they rose above the tallest part of Valhalla, the large stone tower. At the top of the tower, Indy could just make out a solitary figure that raised a spear to the sky in honour of him. Soon, even the tower was lost below them, somewhere beneath the clouds. Still higher the Valkyries flew, as the air grew lighter, Indy began having a hard time breathing. Spots began to cloud his vision until the Valkyries finally stopped their upward momentum.

With a nod at her sisters, Lana was the first to let go. Next was Freyja, who gave a small smile to Indy before winging away. The wind was whistling past the final shield that rested below his body as he began to fall from the sky. Kara looked down at Indy and smiled before kissing him soundly on the lips.

"I have a farewell gift for you, in addition to keeping your necklace..." she said softly, her words almost drown out in the wind. "I was going to keep it as a souvenir of our time together, but I have decided to let it rest with you. I found it the same day I rescued you from the waters of Eden. It was buried within the feathers of my wings. I have kept it safe since that day. I had hoped to give it to you at a better time, maybe as a-

Her words were caught by the wind, but Indy could see the emotion in her eyes. He reached up a hand to stroke Kara's cheek and accepted the gift with his other hand. Kara was crying as she handed over the small wrapped bundle. Indy held her hand a moment longer and gently kissed a pair of heart tattoos on the back of her hand.

With a small nod, she let go of Indy. Her white wings swept out wide and took her away in an instant. Indy clutched his gift to his chest and closed his eyes as he fell from the sky.

Indy fell for what seemed like hours. The panic that held his brain like a vice eased as he began to accept his fate. He played in the air, spinning and floating within the air currents like a stick in the wind. He held onto Kara's gift until his curiosity overwhelmed him and he tore open the simple wrapping. Inside he found a black crystal dragon that shone in the morning sun. Holding it close to his heart Indy continued to drop.

Indy passed through the lowest of the clouds and looked upon the site of his death. He was going to land between the floating Island of Valhalla and a lush green coastline. The ocean would be his grave. Looking around him, he began to pick out more details of the land below him. Indy didn't know if it was a trick of the light or his mind slipping loose but the air on either side of him seemed to shimmer like glitter in the air. An urge to touch the glitter before he died filled him and he moved his arms and legs like sails. The ground was coming up fast now and the glitter was just out of reach. He wasn't going to make it. He was out of time. He stretched even more and at the last second managed to brush the glitter with his outstretched hand before the ocean swallowed him.

Chapter 12 – Eden - Beach Comber

Indy opened his eyes. Waves were beating his body into the sand of the beach but he felt nothing. His entire body was numb and lifeless. He felt like he was in an empty shell of a body and only his mind still lived on. Indy closed his eyes again and waited for his mind to fail. Without a body, a mind could not survive for long, he was sure of that. Minutes rolled by as the surf continued to beat him relentlessly. He was forced to open his eyes, the motion of the ocean was making him sick.

"Can a corpse be sick?" Indy wondered. When he began to laugh to himself his mouth opened and ocean water rushed in. The shock of the water shook some of the fuzziness from his mind. He wasn't dead, he was alive, HE WAS ALIVE! He just couldn't move. Indy strained to move a single muscle in his body. At first, it was his pinkie finger then a toe. Just the effort exhausted him though. Sounds around him were muffled but slowly coming back. He closed his eyes and fell asleep as the ocean continued to wash him.

Something was tugging his arm. Whatever had him was dragging him from the surf and onto the sandy beach. With a groan, Indy pulled free and rolled to his back. A flash of white hopped onto his chest and issued a soft growl. It was a little white wolf.

The white wolf stared down at him with its red eyes and waited. Indy wasn't sure what to do. The little wolf was sitting on his chest and had him pinned to the beach. It was obviously waiting for something.

"INDY!" A voice yelled and was followed by a rush of blonde hair as someone came crashing down on top of him.

"Indy, Indy, Indy," she said. "I thought you were dead! I thought I lost you."

The girl was around his age and had her face pressed to him and was sobbing uncontrollably. She continued to say his name as she wrapped her arms around him and held him tight. It was obvious to him, that this girl knew him. Indy just couldn't bear to tell her that he didn't even know her name. He held on to her as she cried into his shoulder.

"Oh Indy, I am so happy you are alive," she said as the tears continued to roll down her face. "Eden has gone to hell. James and his mercenaries have taken over the castle. But all that needs to wait, the blonde girl took a deep breath and blew it back out again. "Let's get out of the open, the merc's patrol should be by soon."

The young woman stood up and held her hand down to Indy.

"Let's go flyboy."

The girl was willing to help and obviously knew him... and by the way she was acting, cared for him very deeply. Indy accepted her help and together they made their way up the beach to the caves lining the cliffs.

"Adam showed me these caves, they are like a maze of tunnels stretching through the whole ridge. We can get back to Hank's through them."

"Hank?" Indy asked, again not sure of who she was talking about.

"Ya, I know he said he was going to keep out of the fight but he was keeping a little secret in that barn of his. Just wait until we get there, I want it to be a surprise."

Indy followed the girl into the caves and then into the maze of tunnels. She had left a lantern by the tunnel entrance that glowed a soft blue light and as they went, she held his hand.

"We need to be quiet in the tunnels," she whispered. "Adam says that voices carry in here and could alert people to the tunnels existence."

So they travelled the tunnels in silence. Only the glow of the light and the pressure of her hand kept him from becoming lost in the winding caverns.

It took a long time but when the tunnel ahead of them started to lighten, the girl put down her lantern.

"That wasn't so bad was it?" She asked. "Hank's place is just down the road, but we need to go through the woods so we aren't spotted."

Indy nodded and followed her out of the tunnel into a wooded area. Lush green grass and tall trees soared around him. Birdcalls filled the air as they made their way through the woods. A few moments into their hike they could hear a powerful engine approaching. A black and silver car flashed by just feet away from them as the two kids ducked down in behind a fallen tree. The engine noise reverberated in the woods for a few more seconds before it was gone, disappearing into the distance.

"James has been beating that Veyron pretty hard for the last week or so. I think he is making up for lost time." The girl turned to wink at him before rising and continuing towards a large barn in the distance.

"The scientists still have their armour and weapons, so we have them posted as guards in the woods around the barn. They are expecting me, so I doubt they will break cover to come greet us."

There was a large open space between the barn and the woods so they had to run the last stretch of ground. When they reached the barn doors, the girl knocked on the wooden frame twice.

Someone inside called out, "Password."

"Jon you idiot, I know you can see me, open up," she said letting her annoyance seep into her tone.

"You still have to say the password Joslyn. You might be coerced into..." Jon's voice faded away as he opened the door and saw Indy. "Indy?"

"Jon." Indy said with a lopsided grin.

He didn't know the tall lanky kid in front of him, but he was getting used to that.

The girl he now knew as Joslyn spoke up. "I found him washed up on the beach. He is acting a bit spacey but I think he's fine."

"Excellent, get inside though, patrols have been a bit heavier today and Doc is going to want to have a talk with Indy. Man, he is going to flip." Jon smiled as he grabbed them by the arms and pulled them into the barn.

They entered a small room that led into a kitchen area.

"Did you tell him about the..." Jon asked.

"Shhh," Joslyn cut him off. "No, I want it to be a surprise."

"Ha ha, okay cool." Jon said. "Let's go show him the way." Jon led them into the main building of the barn.

The large building was mostly bare inside with only a few rows of machinery and some crates stored in the far corner. They walked to the center of the building where a set of stairs descended a few feet below a large line of machinery. The little walkway was meant as a quick route under the machines to the other side but before they could take the stairs up to the other side, Jon stopped them.

Jon pressed a button labeled "Line Stop". The smooth wall cracked open to reveal another set of stairs leading down.

"Cool eh?" Jon said as he led the way down.

The stairs ended in a large circular room that appeared to be carved from stone. Weapons of all sorts were clustered on racks and tables around the entire circumference of the wall. What really caught Indy's eye was a line of blue light that circled the room like a line of fire. Occasionally the light would ignite a symbol before continue along on its path where it would light a second, different symbol. Indy watched as one of the symbols lit up. It was a circle filled with a pair of crossed swords.

"Valhalla," Indy muttered and watched for the next symbol.

When it lit up it was a circle with a large tree at the center.

Indy didn't remember the name for that symbol, but it looked like the large white tree he had seen as he fell from the sky. Jon and Joslyn were staring expectantly at him from the center of the room.

Jon laughed and said, "He is speechless!"

"There is much more Indy, Adam opened up the tower's top three levels for us to use as we wished." Joslyn said with a little smile. "This is the armoury, the second floor is the main level, where everyone usually meets and the bottom floor is set aside for sleeping. Doc and the others should be on the second floor. We can let Doc get you caught up to speed on everything else."

The second floor was down a curved stairwell at the edge of the room. As they descended, a sense of deja vu came over Indy and he paused on the last step to survey the room. At the center of the room was a large round table surrounded by an odd assortment of chairs. All around the outside of the room were more tables and chairs, along with maps, pictures and drawings.

A small group of men were clustered around one of these boards as they listened to an older man speaking. The grey haired man wore a dirty white lab coat that hung off his bone thin frame. The old man stopped speaking when he saw Indy staring at him from the bottom stair.

"You," the old man said as a hostile look spread over his face. "I thought we had seen the last of you. I guess some things in this world just can't stay dead for long."

"Doc, give him a break," Jon said as he stepped past Indy. "It wasn't his fault and you know it. James is a psychopath, he could have snapped at anything."

"That does not bring my son back, now does it Jonathan." Doc said in a harsh whisper as he approached Indy. "My son is frozen in crystal and I don't know if I will ever get him back. Do you realize how horrific it is to see him staring back at me from within his crystal prison? Do you? I thought not, so why don't you keep your mouth shut while I talk to your friend."

"First thing, have a seat Junior." Doc said as he shoved a rolling chair towards Indy.

The chair rolled all the way to the step and banged off it without Indy even moving a muscle.

Doc huffed impatiently and said, "Fine, if you don't want to be called Junior... Daniel would you take a seat."

"Go ahead Indy, Doc is on our side." Joslyn said with a gentle push. "He is the one keeping us all together and safe. When the castle fell, he was the one that got us all out in one piece."

"Ya, thanks to my secret passages." Jon said annoyed she didn't mention it first.

Indy thought to himself, "How many names did I have?" As he wheeled the chair back to the table and took a seat. He looked up at Doc and waited.

"Okay Daniel, you first, tell us what has happened to you. Where have you been for the last two weeks?" Doc took a seat across the table and leaned forward, eager to hear what had become of Indy.

Indy was confused but by the way everyone was treating him, he was sure he was among friends. Well, except for the guy called Doc. He looked closer at the grey haired man, who clearly an intelligent man. Maybe they might have a clue about getting his memory back.

Indy decided to open up and began from the first thing he could remember. The people around him sat and listened, none of them said a word until Indy had completed his story up to the point Joslyn had found him on the beach.

"So you don't remember any of this? You don't even remember me?" Joslyn said, clearly hurt by the news.

"No, I'm sorry, I don't remember anything before the Valkyrie carried me into Valhalla." Indy said and lowered his gaze. He couldn't stand seeing the hurt look on Joslyn's face.

"Well that explains quite a bit," Doc said. "It seems from young Daniel's description, the force that occupies Eden is nothing but an extremely well-armed group of mercenaries and not the true army of Valhalla. Besides the odd artifact item here and there, we have seen nothing that would lead us to believe this force is anything more than thugs. I am not sure what they are after but I think with a little planning we may be able to encourage them to pack their bags and leave. Especially now we have the Guardian back on our side." Doc's smile was wide but didn't seem to reach his eyes.

Joslyn was eyeing Indy's silver necklace of charms.

"What if we just ripped that whole necklace off? What if those charms are what is causing the memory loss and not some magical potion. Maybe that would restore his memory."

Joslyn slipped her fingers around the chain and was about to pull when Doc placed a hand over hers.

"Like it or not, those charms are a great gift, like his dragon tattoo. We can't afford to take the wrong charm off. If what Indy said is true, his mind is linked to that necklace now, meddling with it could mean losing him entirely. We still don't know if your old boyfriend is even in there anymore. Besides if his story is accurate, Indy is quite the fighter now and that is something I believe may help us in the long run."

Joslyn slowly pulled her hand away and let it drop to her side.

"Fine," she agreed.

"Okay," Indy said. "Get me up to speed on what is going on here. Just a quick overview to help me get my head wrapped around everything."

Doc leaned back in his chair and began to tell Indy about the events surrounding Eden. From the moment he had stepped through the aurora until the Valkyrie whisked him away. After Indy had been taken, Warren had been crystalized by

James. James had gone on to do the same thing to every member of the council as well as Indy's father, Daniel Locke sr. All of the statues were in the castle except for Warren's, which was stored on the third level of the tower, just below them. The castle defense had been broken on the first wave of attackers and had scattered throughout the region. Some people, who didn't manage to escape the mercenary's assault, remained in the castle under guard.

The mercenaries made regular patrols of the area and rounded up any stragglers they found. The Valkyries would occasionally swoop down to take a person that had been injured. Each time one of the Valkyrie took a person, they poured a bit of gold liquid from a flask into the mouth of the captured before winging them away.

"I assume that the golden liquid acts in much the same way as the golden apples. They prevent crystallization during the transit from aurora to aurora. It stands to reason that the liquid or apple may revive the crystal statues. We just haven't been able to obtain any of it for testing purposes. So that will be our first goal, our second will be to rescue those prisoners. The plan on record is to assault the castle tonight after dark. I see no point in delaying the operation. Sasser's group is on overwatch right now and will keep an eye on things until darkness falls. Jon, Joslyn, why don't you get Indy suited up and armed? I will have Sasser meet up with you on the first level at midnight."

Doc stood up from the table and walked away without another word.

"Let's go take a quick look at Warren's statue before we gear up." Jon suggested. "Maybe Indy can think of another way to break people out of the crystal. Something we haven't thought of."

Together they walked down a curving staircase that led to the area the rebels had been using as sleeping quarters. Several sections of rooms had been created by hanging curtains or even sheets from the stone ceiling. The chamber that held Warren's crystal statue also had a large window that was showing images of the world above.

Indy walked up to the crystal statue and was about to place a hand on the back of it when he noticed something staring at him from a side table. It was a little figurine of a bull headed man wearing chainmail. As Indy admired the artwork of the beast, it moved. It stood tall and huffed at him, causing what looked like tendrils of smoke to curl around its black nostrils.

"That's Torn, Doc's little pet Minotaur." Joslyn said as she gave a little whistle. "Don't touch Warren's statue, that little beast gets a little... protective."

Just then a little white wolf raced into the room and pounced into Joslyn's waiting arms.

"And this is Boo."

"Boo?" Indy asked. "That's an odd name for a wolf."

Jon spoke up from the side of Warren's statue. "Dude, don't even ask," he said with a smile that quickly turned into a strangled gasp as Boo leapt at his feet.

The wolf ran past a startled Jon and around the room. On the side table, the Minotaur huffed again and sat back down to watch the kids and Warren.

Indy kept his hand off the sparkling crystal statue and moved around to get a better look at Warren's face. As he moved to the front of the statue, he watched a dark brown eye follow his movements. A smear of white skin peeked through the crystallized skin and glared at Indy with a malevolence that caught him off guard. As Indy inspected the statue, the eye seemed to grow harder and then finally closed in defeat.

"I don't know if this is the same effect as crystalizing outside of the aurora, but if it is, that means if we can get a hold of the liquid James smeared over his eye, we might be able to free anyone in a statue." Jon said as he watched Indy inspect the statue.

"It might even be able to fix this..." Joslyn said as she lifted a frosted hand and brushed several crystalized strands of hair from her face.

Indy looked from the lanky Jon to the beautiful and frosty Joslyn before nodding. "It's worth a shot, what do you have in mind?"

Jon smiled and wrapped an arm around Indy. "Let's go back to the armoury and find a few toys. I've got a plan."

Chapter 13 – Eden - In Ya Go

It was the perfect night for sneaking about. The stars above were concealed by a thick layer of clouds. Indy led the group forward into the night as they ran up the road that snaked up the ridge. Behind him, Jon, Joslyn and Sasser ran silently at his heals as they raced through the night.

Several times, they had to duck off the road when headlights appeared ahead or behind them. When they reached the top of the ridge, they ran out of cover and had to make a mad dash for the shadow of the stone wall. This was the part that was a bit tricky. They had to make it over the wall, undetected, or else the mission would be over before it began. They had brought a few artifacts to help them. The first artifact object came into play a little sooner than expected. A clanging noise echoed through the night seconds before they heard the engine of a car coming through the main gate.

Jon extended a large leather blanket in front of him holding it as high as he could without lifting it off the ground completely. The rest of the group huddled together behind the blanket, trying to stay out of sight. The chameleon cloak worked like a charm and the headlights of the Jeep passed by them without slowing.

"Clear," Jon said as he wrapped the blanket back around his shoulders as a cloak.

Then a second artifact came into play. Joslyn worked a strange bumblebee shaped tube and looked around at the wall in front of them.

"Clear," she whispered.

Everyone had a pair of the third artifact hidden away in a pocket or pouch. Each of them pulled out little green sponges, which were the size of a hockey puck and stuck them to the bottom of their shoes. With one bounce, the little green sponges lifted them into the air. The wall was about ten feet high and was easily cleared by all four people after several bounces.

The only trouble came when they landed from their massive bounce. It took three or four attempts to stop the green sponge's effects. By bending their knees to absorb the landing, each bounce was lessened until they final came to a stop. Jon was the last one to stop bouncing, and Indy had to pull him to the ground or he might have continued to bounce across the grounds.

"Thanks dude," Jon said with a goofy grin. "Those things are pretty wild."

They stored the sponges back in their pockets and ran towards the closest buildings in the complex, a group of landscaping sheds. Sasser popped the lock on the shed with a swift bit of lock picking and ushered them inside. Closing the door silently, they stopped and waited. There was no shout of alarm, no blaring sirens. They had made it in undetected.

After catching their breath, the group began shifting bags of fertilizer until they uncovered a trap door. The door opened quietly and they descended into the darkness below. Joslyn led the way. She reached into her pack to pull out a soft blue light and a small cardboard box. The light illuminated a long dark tunnel ahead. Putting the cardboard box onto the ground, she opened the lid and a little white wolf hopped out and sniffed the air.

The wolf circled the group a couple times playfully before racing off into the dark tunnel ahead. Seconds later a little growl sounded ahead of them. Indy could just make out a pair of red shining eyes ahead.

"Boo says it's clear." Joslyn said and started towards the wolf with the rest of them following in her wake.

The tunnel led all the way up to the cellars of the castle but in several places branched off into the dark. At every intersection, they paused for the wolf to do a quick scout. At last, they came to a panel of wood at the end of the tunnel. Sniffing the wood, the wolf huffed a bit and then sat down on its haunches.

"Are we good?" asked Sasser.

"Not sure," replied Joslyn. "That was a bit of a mixed signal. I am guessing he can't tell for sure, maybe something is throwing his nose off."

Jon spoke up, "Try the telescope. The room is a bit close but we should be able to see most of it."

Joslyn pulled out the bumblebee shaped artifact and checked the room. She continued to scan until she was absolutely sure no one was in sight.

"Looks clear guys," she confirmed.

"Okay, let me go first, prep your weapons, and try to keep quiet." Indy said as he slid a pair of heavy weighted gloves over his hands. Follow my lead and whatever you do, don't shoot anyone unless you have to."

Indy looked directly at Sasser, who had been the only one of them that decided to bring a gun with them.

Jon pulled a long sword from a scabbard at his back and Joslyn unslung a long tube that she had brought, keeping a short silver sword in its sheath at her hip. From a case on her other hip, she pulled out several darts and placed them in a small holder near the end of the tube. Each dart was coated with a liquid Doc Hocking had provided. One dart was enough to drop a mountain lion, or so they had been assured.

Indy pushed on the panel and it slid open revealing the castle's wine cellar. As Indy stepped down from the open portal, the white wolf rushed past, almost making him lose his footing. The wolf ghosted into the cellar silent as can be. Checking around the room once, Indy motioned for the others to follow.

A thud sounded behind Indy and he turned to see a mercenary in black holding a knife in one hand, lying on the ground. The mercenary was face down and out cold. The white wolf sat beside the merc and let its red-eyed gaze settle on Indy for a moment before disappearing again into the dark room.

Joslyn nodded and gave Indy a little smile.

"Nice puppy," Indy said with a grin.

They made their way through the cellars, checking for other hidden surprises, but found none.

"Okay," Sasser whispered. "My scouts watching the castle report that the prisoners have been using the kitchen doors quite frequently.

My guess is that the soldiers are using them as manual labour, cooking, cleaning and what not. So, with any luck, we can grab one or two and give them a little interrogation. Our priority is the golden ale, followed by getting a few of the prisoners out if we can. If we are spotted we drop whatever we are doing and run."

They went up the stairs and into the hallway outside the kitchens, the white wolf had disappeared from view, so they had to take extra care scouting the path. Indy could hear pots and pans banging in the kitchen as they approached. But, when they heard footsteps coming their way, they had to all cram into a nearby panty closet. Peeking through the crack in the door Indy saw an odd sight. A young man and woman were coming down the hallway holding a large lump of amber crystal in their hands. At second glance, the crystal wasn't really being held, it was completely enveloping their hands. Indy looked closer at the pair and noticed other things about them as well. It was something about their hair, it glittered in the light of the hall and was the same color as the crystal binding their hands together. Even the thick stubble on the young man's square chin glittered with the amber crystal. The pair of teenagers looked beaten and exhausted, their eyes downcast as they moved down the hall. The young man had a sack of flour over his shoulder, while the younger woman was carrying a tray filled with metal steins and a large jug. As luck would have it, they were not being accompanied by a guard.

Indy moved into the hall with his group following close behind.

"Thomas, Amber," Jon said as he saw the pair. "Quick, come with us."

The two teenagers stopped abruptly at the first sight of Indy coming through the door. When they heard Jon's words, they started to laugh. A strange odd cackling laugh came from their mouths and everyone stopped in their tracks as the noise echoed through the hallway.

Thomas looked at Indy and said, "The master has been..."

Amber finished the sentence, "...waiting for you. He knew it..."

"...was just a matter of time..." Thomas said.

"...before you came back." Amber finished.

The strange pair talked as if they were one person. Even their voices sounded eerily the same.

Together the pair took a deep breath and started to yell, "Guar-

Indy called out to Joslyn, "Dart Amber."

He took two quick strides to the pair as a little huff echoed behind him. A little rose of color blossomed at the base of Amber's throat as Indy's heavy fist connected with Thomas's jaw. Indy's punch created a shower of amber coloured crystals as Thomas's beard hair shattered. The odd pair crumbled in a heap and Indy just managed to grab the jug before it fell. However, the sack of flour landed hard and split apart in a cloud. The hallway was instantly filled with the choking white powder and amber dust. Indy emerged from the cloud with the large stein of ale. The stein was adorned with images of Valkyries in flight and its lid was decorated with the crossed swords of Valhalla.

"I poured the ale from the jug into this stein, that should keep it from spilling out for now but we have to move fast," Indy said quickly. "We can't trust those two with the secret of the tunnels, just in case they escape. I think we have what we came for."

Indy held up the stein of ale and opened it to show his companions, the golden liquid inside sloshing around with the movement.

Sasser nodded and said, "Either way we have to go, Doc can run some tests on it to make sure. Follow me."

They turned and ran for the wine cellar, as sirens starting going off around the castle. Luck was with them again as they made their way back to the secret panel and out into the tunnels.

"I think we should put the sponges on now." Joslyn suggested, "We might not have time to stop at the wall."

"Good idea," Jon said and smiled widely. "Just make sure you catch me on the other side."

The green sponges on the bottom of their shoes made the trip up and over the wall comical. Every step they took was enhanced, so one stride turned into a leap. Each leap grew longer and higher as they raced. One after the other they crossed the grounds, each of them making the ten-foot leap over the wall easily. Joslyn was the last one left in the shed, she was waiting for the wolf that hadn't returned. She put the wolf's cardboard box on the ground and waited. Indy stopped just short of the wall and was waiting for her there. Joslyn was still in the shed when the outside floodlights lit up. Overhead a helicopter buzzed by and the roar of Jeeps coming up the road filled the night.

"Stay put Joslyn," Indy called. "Head back into the tunnels, I will come back for you tomorrow night."

There wasn't much he could do for her right now, except to create a distraction. Joslyn waved in acknowledgment and closed the shed door. From the other side of the wall he could hear Sasser's voice.

"We have to go Indy."

"Go ahead, I am going to draw them off. I will meet you at Hank's." Indy said as he slid another artifact from his pack.

He had found it among the piles of artifacts in the tower of Eden. It was a long stick, almost like Joslyn's blowgun, but slightly wider. Jon had told him it had been a favourite artifact of Warren's. It was also the perfect distraction maker.

As the helicopter buzzed by overhead, Indy took careful aim and then blew into one end of the tube. A stream of red, orange and yellow fireworks shot out and streaked by the front of the helicopter. The helicopter turned in the air to locate the source of the fireworks.

Just to be sure he had gotten their attention, Indy blew into the tube again. This time the result was a little more spectacular. The helicopter had just rotated sideways and opened a side door as the stream hit. The fireworks entered the open helicopter door and exploded inside. Lights and smoke poured out of every crack and crevice of the chopper. It began spinning around in midair as its engines whined in protest. Faster and faster, it spun until the pilot inside lost control. The chopper spiralled down to the ground and crashed through the landscaping shed where Joslyn had been hiding.

The breath caught in Indy's throat as he realized what he had done. Jeeps were coming at him from across the compound and he had to hope that Joslyn had made it back into the tunnel in time. Indy bounded away as the green sponges did their thing. He was up and over the wall in seconds. Keeping visible, he stayed on the road where the sponges could get the most bounce. Once he lost his pursuers, he would circle back to the tower.

Indy made it back to Hank's in good time, having long lost his pursuit along a set of overgrown railway tracks. None of the Jeeps could pass through this heavily overgrown area and Indy was easily able to disappear into the night. When he entered the second level of the tower all eyes in the room turned to him. Without speaking, he simply hefted the mug of ale. Cheers erupted around him and Doc Hocking rushed forward to take the mug.

"Good work Daniel," he said with a curt nod of his head. "I will perform some experiments on the liquid to see if it can be replicated. I will be in my lab."

Doc practically ran down the stairs leading to the third level without looking back. Jon and Sasser waved Indy over to a private conference they were having.

"Glad to see you made it back Indy." Jon said quietly. "But what about Joslyn? What are we going to do?"

"I told her I would go back for her tomorrow night. I don't care if Doc has the juice ready in time or not." Indy's voice rose as his anger started to boil again.

Doc Hocking had a lot of work to do. Now that he had his hands on the golden liquid, the first thing he needed to do was try it on his son. Running down the stairs of the tower to the third level, he made his way to his section of the room. They had been using sheets for walls in order to afford each other a bit of privacy. His room had one of the six windows on this level and in front of the window, he had placed his son's crystal statue. Currently the magical windows were dark and empty. Warren's one good eye was focused on the darken window as

Doc came in, holding the stein of ale up like a trophy.

"I have it Warren. I have it," Doc assured his son as he opened the top of the stein to reveal the golden liquid.

Dipping one finger into the liquid, he rubbed it across Warrens frozen lips. Instantly the crystal melted away, leaving Warren's mouth clear of the crystal.

"Dad," Warren mumbled, the crystal around his face preventing his mouth from opening properly. "Help me..."

Without another word, Doc tilted the stein to his son's lips. He poured the golden liquid into Warren's mouth until it started to dribble down his chin.

"Swallow it Warren," Doc said in a hushed voice, not daring to breathe as he waited.

Warren closed his one good eye as the liquid slid down his throat. The crystal skin that had imprisoned Warren's body evaporated from sight. Warren fell to the ground as the last bit of crystal faded away. Worried, Doc rushed over to check on Warren's vital signs. Everything checked out and Doc issued a sigh of relief. Taking great care, he lifted his son from the floor and carried him to the nearest bed.

"Sleep now son," Doc urged. "I am sure you will wake once you have recovered."

Doc turned off the lights in the room and pulled up a chair to the bedside. There he sat staring down at his son, a wide smile plastered over his lips.

The tower was abuzz with the news that the golden liquid had revived Warren. Doc had still not left his son's side, but had told them that his son was doing well. He expected a full recovery and gave the golden liquid his seal of approval. So the mission was a go, they would attempt a rescue of the prisoners, trapped councillors and Indy's father. Now that they had a way to combat the crystal orbs James had used, the E.D.T. would be on a more level playing field.

Scientists had dropped what they were doing upon hearing the news and began gathering their armour and weapons. Within minutes, there was a room full of awkward men in shining artifact armour. Sasser began drawing up plans, as they prepared for their mission. He had sent scouts out to monitor the castle and had been receiving reports all morning.

It turned out that the mercenaries had already started preparing to leave the castle. Scouts reported that several of the ships on the coast had already departed. Stacks of boxes, crates and other supplies had been taken down to the beach and were being shuttled out of Eden as well.

The biggest piece of news came in later that day. The U.S.S. Herald had arrived and parked itself just outside the shadow of Valhalla. Jet fighters had begun circling the skies outside of the aurora and there were other signs of a massive military build-up in the area. However, it was the last report that came into the tower that worried Indy the most.

Sasser read the report aloud for Indy and Jon, "Scouts have reported seeing the mercenaries carrying crystal statues up onto the castle's roof. It looks like they are being arranged for a possible airlift. Several statues have already been sealed in large wooden shipping boxes. James has also been spotted patrolling the roof, looking up at the sky."

Sasser looked up from his report to the two young men.

"Looks like it's now or never Indy and since Doc isn't leaving his son's side, we are going to need a leader. It needs to be someone strong. Someone everyone here can trust, someone that has been named Guardian not too long ago."

Indy looked taken aback by the obvious suggestion. He quickly recovered when he realized more than one person was watching for his reaction, waiting for an answer. One quick nod sealed the deal. He would lead them all back to the castle to save the councillors... and his father. Sasser passed the scouts reports into Indy's hand and put his hand on Indy's shoulder.

"Your plan, your way," Sasser said softly. "Just remember, there are lives at stake here, not all of these people have bulletproof skin."

Indy nodded and looked down at the papers in his hand to give his mind time to form a plan. Several times, he looked up from the papers to see the others waiting on his words. Men, women and kids. He even spotted someone he recognized. A large old man had just come up from the lower level and was making his way to the next set of stairs.

"Hank?" Indy asked, not sure if the name fit at first, a memory stirred in the back of his mind.

But as the name rolled off his tongue, he was sure.

"Hank!" Indy practically shouted the name with glee. "I remember you Hank."

Something was wrong about the man though, Indy realized as the memory of the man started to slip away. It was like trying to hold water in his fist, the harder he tried to hang onto it and the faster the memory started to slip away. In the end, Indy was only left with the man's name and a warm sense of familiarity and kinship.

The old farmer standing on the stairs of the tower smiled in acknowledgement and then waved goodbye.

"Sorry I can't be a part of this," Hank said in a loud gravelly voice.

Indy ran over to the big farmer and hugged him tight. Remembering his old friend's name had sent shivers through his body and put a smile on his lips.

"I won't ask you to come with us Hank, I can see you don't want to go... but why? I thought my dad was your friend."

Hank lowered his voice to a rough whisper.

"I promised my Mag's that I would never involve myself in any kind of violence and I keep my promises."

Hank turned to leave but said over his shoulder, "I left you some cider though, and a little note from a friend. It's down in Jon's room."

"Cider?" Jon's ears practically stood straight up upon hearing that one magic word. "In my room? Thanks Hank!"

Jon was up and running in a heartbeat.

"Thank you Hank," Indy held out his hand and the big farmer engulfed it with his own. "We couldn't have gotten through this mess without you."

"Goodbye Indy," Hank said releasing his hand. "I don't think I will be seeing you for a while, so take care. Oh, and take care of Little Cloud too. Tell her... aww never mind."

The big man nodded once at Indy and walked up the steps and out of view.

Indy's memory was a bit fuzzy about what was so special about the cider, but he knew from Jon's reaction that if he were to have any chance of having any, he would have to hurry.

Jon had drunk half of a large glass pitcher of cider before Indy was able to make it down to the lower level. A broad smile covered Jon's face as he slumped back in a chair and sighed deeply.

"Man this stuff is good. Go on Indy, give it a go. You might not remember, but this is the best cider you will ever taste."

Indy poured himself a glass and took a deep sip. Jon was right, it was the best... Indy sputtered and coughed. Apple cider rushed out of his mouth and down his chin. It was as if someone had flicked a light switch in his brain. He remembered. He remembered everything. The look on his face must have alerted Jon to the sudden change.

"Indy, you okay dude?" He asked. "You look... a bit weird."

Indy gave Jon a lopsided grin and punched him in the shoulder... hard.

"That is for hitting my cast."

Jon's face screwed up in thought as he rubbed his shoulder.

"I didn't hit you that hard..."

Then sudden realization flooded though him.

"You remember? You remember! That is awesome! I can't believe it... was it the cider? I knew it was good but oh man... Good old Hank."

Indy nodded once and poured more of the sweet cider into his mouth. This time he didn't spit it out, instead savouring the sweet thick liquid. He noticed a note on the same table as the pitcher of cider. Picking it up, Indy opened the note and read.

Dear Indy,

By now you have had a sip of the cider, if not, put this note down until you do.

The cider you are drinking has been altered slightly at my hands. Don't worry it's still the same great cider you know and love. I have just added a little something extra to kick-start your old memories. The charms you are wearing are a great treasure and should be held in the highest of regard. The necklace will continue to work its magic and should be considered a very valuable tool in the future. The charms are not linked to your memory loss, the golden leaves of one of the white trees are. Valkyries use these leaves as a subtle form of control over new acquisitions, to make their transition into Valhalla a little easier. Fortunately for you, you drank the Valkyrie's mixture while still under the protection of the dragon tattoo. That slight interference may have saved you from a more permanent memory loss.

Now that you have regained your memory, I feel it is time to share a few things with you. I am sorry I am not able to visit you in person, but rest assured, it is nothing personal. I have been keeping a close eye on the situation and it is going better than I expected when Valhalla first arrived. The mercenaries have not been able to locate the missing piece of compass, which would have led them straight to the tower of Eden. I am not sure where you have hidden it myself but I am glad that they were denied.

The military build-up outside of the aurora has grown quite large and I am afraid a confrontation is imminent. I have re-created several of the sleds you have enjoyed flying in the past, to aid you in your quests. You can find them on the level below when you are ready to go. To open that level, simply say my name three times.

-Your little friend

P.S. Your gift is finally ready, it took quite a bit of convincing, but I think it should stay with you for a little while at least.

"ADAM, ADAM, ADAM!" Indy shouted.

Of course, Jon looked at him as if he had just gone off the deep end.

A rumble sounded not far from Jon's room and Indy raced toward the noise. A new stairwell had opened up to another lower level. Indy took the stairs three at a time as lights blossomed around the new area below. The room was the same as the others above, circular and made of stone. What excited Indy the most was the five A.G.P. sleds at the center of the room. Each gleaming black sled was arranged in a star pattern, facing into the center of the room. At the center, on the floor was a large glowing emblem. The symbol for the tower of Eden, a large glowing tree surrounded by a circle of blue. At the center of the emblem was a small black winged creature. Some kind of shredded red ribbon was hanging from one corner of its mouth and scattered in little mounds all around its clawed feet.

As Indy approached, the little dragon raised itself on its two hind legs and roared. Well, it tried to roar, the thing sounded more like a little cat purring. A few beats of its wings lifted the dragon into the air. Winging its way around the room, it flew at Indy and landed on his shoulder.

"What is it with you people and your pets." Jon complained. "Don't we have enough things to worry about without having to deal with more animals?"

The dragon hissed its disapproval at Jon and then winged around the room again to land on one of the A.G.P.s.

"Sweet," Jon said as he looked dreamily at the sleds.

Doubt crossed his face as he looked at Indy and shook his head.

"You better not to wreck these ones like you did the last two you flew."

Laughing they both climbed into the sleds and activated them. The little black dragon took off like a rocket as the sleds started up. It winged its way up the stairs and out of sight.

Indy and Jon looked at each other with wide smiles before lifting off in pursuit of the dragon. It was going to be fun seeing the look on everyone's face as they drove up and out of the tower on the sleds.

Chapter 14 - Eden / Valhalla – Girl Troubles

Joslyn quickly shut the shed door as the helicopter buzzed by overhead. Indy had promised that he would come back for her tomorrow night. She would just have to sit tight until then. It was frustrating to have to wait for him to save her... again. She was so fed up with the whole damsel in distress thing.

"Hffft" she huffed into the dark and raised her hand to the shed door.

"I can run just as fast as them, those soldiers will be distracted now anyway."

She was just about to open the door when the sounds of explosions went off around the shed.

"Forget that plan!" She yelled and backed away from the door.

A thud sounded behind her as the trap door was struck from below.

"They found the tunnel," she thought in horror as the trap door thudded again.

She was just turning for the door when she heard the scratching and whining coming from below.

"Boo!" She cried and lifted the trap door open. In the darkness below sat her little white wolf. "Boo, you scared me! Come here Boo."

Joslyn patted her thigh. The wolf refused to budge. It started to whine again before dashing away into the tunnels below.

"Boo wait! Don't leave me."

Joslyn jumped down into the tunnel and ran after the wolf. An instant after she left the shed, something crashed through it. A muffled explosion blew her from her feet and she skidded to a rest on the tunnel floor. Debris scattered around her and pinned her to the ground as part of the tunnel collapsed around her.

When the dust settled, she opened her eyes to the white wolf licking her face.

"Stop, stop Boo. I'm okay."

Joslyn grabbed her little friend in a fierce hug. The little wolf continued to lick her face a bit longer before breaking free and dancing away. The wolf turned in a circle and came back to her as Joslyn was getting up from the ground. The wolf grabbed the little sack tied around Joslyn's neck and pulled.

"I know we can' stay here boo. Go ahead, you lead the way, maybe we can sneak out the kitchen's side door." Joslyn said as she tried to brush the wolf aside.

Boo continued to tug on the little bag necklace until the bag finally ripped off completely. Then the little wolf dashed off with the bag clutched firmly in its mouth.

"Now is not the time for games you little thief."

Joslyn was just about to tuck the now exposed section of compass back into her shirt when she realized she could see. The lantern had been left behind in the shed but something around her was giving off a soft blue light. Lifting up her necklace, she found the source of the light. It was the half-moon of metal Indy had given her for safekeeping. One of the emblems on its surface was lit with the blue light. The blue light flickered and died as she turned the piece of metal over in her hands. As she returned it to its original position and it lit up again. Joslyn moved the scrap of metal around some more as she circled in place. When she was done, Joslyn had the little compass figured out. As long as the symbol for Eden was pointing in the proper direction. It didn't matter where she was, this thing would lead her back to the tower.

Joslyn started to jog down the tunnel chasing after Boo with the compass lighting her way. She hadn't gotten far when she came across Boo standing at a crossroad in the tunnel. The wolf had its hackles raised as it stood staring off down the tunnel towards the castle. The wolf silently slipped down a side passage and whined when Joslyn didn't immediately follow.

Footsteps echoed down the hallway ahead of her a second before Joslyn slid down the side passage to follow her wolf. They were only ten feet from the crossing when the wolf stopped her with a tug on her pant leg. Joslyn looked down through the blue light to look at the wolf.

"Oh no, the light." Joslyn said, turning the compass away from Eden and immediately the light faded. In the darkness, she barely dared to breathe as the footsteps came closer. She turned to look down the hallway and saw a soft light envelope the passage. She knelt down and hugged the side of the wall as a figure passed by the mouth of her tunnel. Then the footsteps stopped. It was silent and still in the tunnel and Joslyn was sure the man that had just went by could hear the pounding of her heart.

A voice spoke ahead of her that she recognized immediately as James.

"Colonel Tapper, do you copy," James said.

A radio crackled softly before a southern drawl came over the radio.

"Tapper here, report."

"The tunnels are clear, looks like the intruders have gotten away. Reports are coming in, we have several men injured and one helicopter down.

"And still you are no closer to discovering the other tower. You disappoint me James. I was assured you could locate the wish box, without it this whole incident is a farce."

"Sorry sir, I assumed that the tower would be in the same location as before, just below ground.

"Assuming can be a very unhealthy trait for certain people."

"Please Sir, just give me one more day, if I can find the missing piece of the compass, the treasures of Eden will be ours. I just need more time."

"You are out of time James, I am proceeding with an alternative plan now. There are three unlit emblems left on the compass in my possession, since the white box here is unavailable to us now, we shall seek another."

"You still need me to tell Odin where to move the island," James said in a low voice.

"That is not completely accurate now." Tapper laughed. "Tsu is now a Guardian of Valhalla as well, Odin will listen to him as readily as you."

James went silent on the radio but took a deep breath and cursed loudly. The radio squawked with Tappers voice, this time broadcasting to all units.

"All personnel, Attention all personnel. Evacuation plan alpha is a go. Repeat alpha is a go."

The radio squawked again as it switched channels.

"You have twelve hours to get your affairs in order James. We will speak more when you return to Valhalla. Colonel Tapper out."

"You old fool!" James swore and a thud echoed through the tunnel.

His footsteps raced back the way he came and the light faded from the tunnel.

"That was a close one, hey Boo?" Joslyn said as she pointed the Eden emblem to the south and its glow returned to light the tunnel. "I don't know about you, but I don't think heading back to the castle is a great idea anymore."

The wolf responded by dashing away into the dark unexplored section of tunnel. Joslyn lifted the glowing piece of metal and followed the wolf.

The tunnel she was in wound its way through the earth for miles until she came to a small door. The door was unlocked and she pushed through it into a small rocky cave. As soon as she opened the door, she could hear waves crashing in the distance and the smell of salt water filled her nose.

Boo hopped through the door and raced off into the cave. Now it was just a matter of making her way back to Hank's place. Joslyn followed the wolf out of the caves and onto the beach.

The ocean spread out before her as she walked along the sand. The massive floating island dominated the sky to the west and the briar thorn wall rose up around the Aurora California to the south. The ridge behind her was a cliff face that was going to be a very difficult climb so she started to wander further to the south following the coast towards the briar wall. The wall was full of thick thorns that covered every inch of every vine. There would be absolutely no climbing this beast of a barrier. The thorns would rip her to shreds.

Turning to look around the area Joslyn was beginning to feel frustrated. A sharp huff from Boo grabbed her attention. The white wolf had been frolicking in the bushes nearby but came running to her side and stood with its hackles raised. Joslyn turned to see what had set her friend off. There on an outcropping of rocks was an extremely large mountain lion. The big cat sat still and silent as it glared at her, waiting for her to flee. Joslyn reached for the sword at her hip as the cat began to pounce.

The cat hit the sandy beach five feet from her and Boo lunged to intercept it. As they collided, the big cat was deflected from its path and passed Joslyn just a few feet to her right. Boo went sprawling across the sand and lay unmoving. The mountain lion spun around to face Joslyn and started to hiss. Boo had bought her several precious seconds and enabled Joslyn to get her sword free and ready. The cat leapt at her again and Joslyn swung the sword with all her might. Claws raked across her throat as the sword bit hard into the mountain lion's side.

They tumbled together in a heap and crashed down onto the beach. The cat was above her and had her pinned but the animal wasn't moving. It wasn't even breathing. Joslyn coughed once and then tried to free herself from under the cat. The big animal was unmovable and she was quickly running out of strength. Her head started to swim and her vision began to darken. The darkness seemed to grow until the world around her disappeared. Then there was only darkness.

A voice spoke to her in her dreams. "She is a strong one."

"Yes she is, and she is very pretty."

"Odin will approve, but look... the wound is already healing. Eden is still protecting this one. The blue glow of that necklace is proof enough of that."

"Let her choose her path after it is done. She will be stronger if she is willing."

"No one has ever rejected the gift."

"Yes but none of us have much to return to. Unlike us, if this one returns, she will have a whole body, badly scarred, but whole."

"And what of the crystallization damage, will it persist upon ascension."

"That I do not know, give her the ale, we shall soon find out."

A small silver flask wrapped with golden leaves appeared before Joslyn's face and was pressed to her lips. Then a fire burned through her and a tingling numbness set in over her heart.

A scream passed through her lips as the blood loss finally caught up to her and her adrenaline faded. Something around her neck was choking her, cutting off her air and making the world around her go dark.

In her dreams, Joslyn was being fed honey and crusty bread by a woman with dark eyes and a crown of feathers. In the dream, Joslyn seemed to fade in and out of consciousness. Darkness was pressing in all around her and only a few soft glowing lights above gave her comfort. Under her body the ground bulged against her, at times feeling like it was heaving like an earthquake. Her arms and legs couldn't move, she was frozen in place as the world around her darkened again and the lights disappeared.

When Joslyn finally woke, she was laying on the ground at the base of a great white tree with golden leaves. The sunlight streamed through the branches above as the leaves danced in a light breeze. She could see several black ravens in the branches above her and several larger white birds higher up. Six women knelt around her with their heads bowed and lips moving. Each one of the women was wearing a feathered circlet and a feathery cloak around their shoulders. Three white on her left and three black on her right. Both of Joslyn's hands were being held by two of the beautiful women.

"Where am I?" Joslyn asked.

Her mouth was dry but her voice seemed... different to her own ears. It was... firmer... stronger.

The woman holding her right hand looked up and smiled.

"Good morning, I am Freyja, your sister."

The woman on her left spoke up, "I am Kara, and I too am your sister."

"All of the Valkyries are now your sisters." Freyja said. "Rise now Mist and spread your wings."

As if on cue, the feathery cloaks lifted off the women's shoulders and raised high into the air as wings. In response, the uncomfortable feeling in Joslyn's back rippled and with a burst of pain, tore free from beneath her. Something from below her forced Joslyn to sit up straight. Wings rose up over her head and spread wide. The women around her stared in awe and then in confusion.

"That is impossible," Freyja said, her mouth gaping wide in disbelief.

Joslyn looked back over her shoulder and saw a pair of black wings that had ripples of white feathers layered within them. Confusion clouded her mind as she looked to the other Valkyries for an explanation.

Kara grabbed one of her shoulders.

"It's okay Mist. You're okay, just take a few deep breaths and try to relax. The memory loss you are experiencing is normal. Your name is Mist, you are one of us now, a Valkyrie."

"What the heck are you talking about? My name is Joslyn. What kinda stunt are you wackos trying to pull. And what's with the fake angel wings, aren't they a bit much?"

Joslyn reached up to tug a wing and cursed loudly when pain shot down her new wing unexpectedly.

"You remember your old name... that is impossible. The ceremony removes all lingering aspects of your old life and marries you to the essence of the Valkyrie. The silver water you drank is our essence and eating the golden bowl of leaves removes your memories."

"But Freyja, look at her wings, the essence is supposed to choose an aspect, raven or swan. Not both!"

Freyja considered the wings and inspected Joslyn's bright blue eyes. This is quite an unexpected gift you have been granted Mist... I mean Joslyn. Odin must have something special in mind for you, your future must be very great indeed."

Freyja put a hand on Joslyn's shoulder and patted her gently.

"For the moment, I want you to assume your new name. Lana will guide you as a mentor, until we can figure out this little dilemma. Until then I ask that you please try to keep a low profile."

"But I have wings!" Joslyn said in amazement as she experimentally shook her wings out.

"Go slowly Mist. You will be weak for a time as your body continues to transform and strengthen. Until then you need to stay near the tree or the pond. Either one will help sustain you now."

A thought crossed Joslyn's mind and burst from her lips. "Indy, you did this to Indy too! You fed him one of those golden leaves and made him forget. How could you... you monsters."

Joslyn tried to stand but there was no strength in her limbs. The effort of moving that much tired her severely and sleep started to overcome her. Her eyelids grew heavy and threatened to close.

Before she was out, she heard Kara's voice. "Indy? My chosen? Mist, does he still live... Mist! Is Indy still alive?"

"Let her sleep, Kara. She has a long road ahead of her, you can get your answers later."

Chapter 15 – Eden - Up on the Rooftop

Five sleek black shapes flitted over the treetops at top speed. The ground blurred beneath Indy as he and Jon led the three other sleds toward the castle. The little dragon had stayed behind at the tower and no amount of convincing could get the little beast to follow him. Indy watched the ground as he stretched out and felt a twinge in the pit of his belly as the A.G.P. started to rise higher over the treetops.

Everyone, save for Indy, was outfitted in the best artifact armour they could find and their choice of weapons. Jon had elected for a long sword, while Indy had found a pair of the dragon sticks that he had been so fond of. Behind them flew Jon's father, Barney, Blake Sanders and Michael Hacker. Blake and Michael were part of the science team that had first used the armour suits against the Chinese mercenaries.

All three of the adults carried purple energy whips that had been so effective before. The plan was to drop onto the castle's roof and take control of the area while Jon administered the golden crystal ale to the councillors. Once free from their statues the survivors would be shuttled back to the tower. With any luck, the mercs wouldn't spend too much time trying to track them down. Indy hoped that they would be too busy trying to get back to Valhalla and away from the military might that was assembling in the Pacific Ocean.

The first part of their plan went off perfectly. They landed the sleds on the roof and took up positions guarding all ways onto the roof. Jon then started prying open the boxes. Before he could even get one box open, a whistling noise came hurtling through the air.

"Take cover, RAVENS!" Indy shouted.

The black bird came in way too fast for Jon to react. In slow motion, it released the whistling spear held in its talons. The silver spear streaked towards Jon and buried itself deep into his shoulder.

"Nooo!" Indy ran to Jon's side in time to cradle his friends landing as he fell.

Barney was a heartbeat later and took up his son's hand.

"Jon, Jon, can you hear me? Speak to me son. Please..."

Jon didn't respond, his wide eyes stared off into the sky. An explosion rocked the roof top as the doorway to the main stairs ripped open.

James and a handful of merc's came storming onto the roof.

"Barney, we have to go, there is nothing we can do for him right now." Indy said as he laid Jon's head down on the stone roof.

Barney looked at Indy with a cold dead glare.

"Kill them all," Barney said as he turned from his son's body and attacked the soldiers coming on to the roof.

Indy chased after his best friend's father as his blood began to boil and his rage over took him once again. Indy tapped his dragon sticks together twice and they ignited with a blue light. It was four against ten but of the people standing against them, only James held any real power. Indy and Barney crashed into the soldiers and amid the gunfire dispatched them in seconds.

The same could not be said about Blake and Michael. They had squared off against James. Darkness rolled around James like shadows of fire. The dark helmet on his head seemed to absorb the light around him. In his hand, he held a long stick capped with a white glowing ball. With a casual flick of the wrist, the glowing ball broke free of the stick and struck Blake in the chest. With another slight motion, James flicked his wrist again. The white ball moved high into the air with Blake still attached. Michael moved in to help save Blake. His purple whip snaked out and struck at James, coiling itself around his feet. A second later, the whip crackled with electricity as it coursed down the rope and into James.

Purple fire seemed to envelope James but he paid it no mind. Instead, he began swinging Blake around like he was a balloon. Tiring of the display James released him. Blake fell from the sky and down past the roof to the ground, out of sight.

The small globe of light returned to the stick James held with a flick of the wrist. He looked down at the whip entwining his ankles and laughed. Kicking himself free from the purple rope, James stalked towards Michael. Darkness flowed from his helmets eyes as he stood above the now cowering scientist.

"I think you have made your last mistake, fool."

James reared back and kicked the man in the head dropping him flat. Pulling a crystal orb from a pouch at his waist, James crushed it into the man's chest. Crystal formations spread out from the orb and covered Michael within seconds.

Indy could see all this happening as he battled with the soldiers. The dragon sticks hummed and twirled as mercenaries fell. Around him, the bodies of nine men lay moaning.

"Barney, get out of here, there is nothing you can do against James. Let me handle it."

Barney didn't hear a single word Indy had said. Instead, he ran for James. The suit of armour glinted in the sunlight as he attacked. Barney threw punches and kicks at James in an endless rage. James stood there and took it all, every single punch. But there was no apparent effect. Barney wore himself down in a matter of seconds and collapsed, his chest heaving.

James reached down, picked Barney up by the neck, and casually tossed him from the roof. Indy's breath caught in his throat as Jon's dad went over the side, but he relaxed as he realized the artifact armour would protect him from the fall.

"Now that we are alone we can have a nice little chat, brother." James said as he took his helmet off and dropped it on the floor. "Put those silly little sticks down you know they can't hurt me."

Indy knew he was right, James had the same kind of tattoo shield he had. The only thing Indy had found capable of inflicted damage on either one of them was the angel sword. That sword was lost to them now, probably in a pile of dust where he had crashed his first sled. Indy let the sticks in his hands fall and crossed his arms. He would hear James out and then he would wipe the floor with his smug little face, for John and all his other friends this monster had hurt.

"I know how things look right now, brother, but you need to understand... it's not my fault." James's hard expression softened a bit as he spoke. "I have been living in your shadow for years now, when I was younger I sent dad a note saying who I was and that all I wanted was to meet him. Daniel rejected me, flat out denied my existence, and even threatened my mother. He swore that if she ever dared bring me to America he would ruin her life. Do you know what he did next? He bought her off, he paid her one million dollars to tell me that she was mistaken, that he wasn't the actual father. Do you believe that? I tell you what, a million U.S. dollars goes a long way in Korea. I had the best education money could buy, I had extensive training in anything and everything I could find a coach for. I have three different black belts and can speak seven different languages, thanks to dad. But when a car accident killed my mom, I was left an orphan. I had no idea who my father was except for a vague recollection about one Daniel Locke sr. I worked my way into his organization and rung by rung, I climbed his corporate ladder. It took a few years but I was finally able to get what I wanted, proof that he was my father. During one of the staff meetings I was able to get some DNA evidence that spelled out for certain he was my father. I scheduled a meeting with him to shove that little piece of paper down his throat... the funny thing was he didn't show. It was your mom, Jolie that turned up in his place. When I showed her the evidence, she actually hugged me. She sat me down and talked to me like I was part of the family but she also gave me a warning. She said that my father would never recognize me as his son. If I told him the truth, he would send me away without a second thought. I would never be welcomed as part of the family. I was heartbroken to say the least, however your mother had a solution. She offered me an alternative. I would be accepted into the family as a personal servant, allowed to participate in family life and be near my father. She said that there would come a day when he would need me, and that if I proved myself, he would accept me for who I really was. She told me it was my choice, and that she would be my advocate no matter which path I chose."

"So what took so long then?" Indy asked. "How come you didn't come forward sooner?"

James looked down for a moment before speaking.

"I made a mistake. I trusted the wrong man with the wrong information. Once he had something on me, the situation snowballed. At first, it was nothing, some little tidbit of information here, a piece of paper there. Sometimes it would just be dad's schedule. It was always more and more though, I guess the biggest thing I did wrong was the product leak. I was under pressure to come up with something and that day dad really bit my head off for no reason. So to get back at him..."

"You stole the prototype." Indy said bluntly.

"Ya, I did, and once they had that one on me, my life was over. They had me over a barrel and there was no way out. I was going to prove to dad I had what it took and that I wasn't trying to be his son just for the money. I had it all set up, a corporation to run, a new fresh product to bring to market. I had a shot, a real shot to make it big.

"So that is all well and good but you need to explain the whole shooting my dad in the leg thing... and what about inside the tower. You were going to shoot Joslyn and you beat the crap out of Hank."

"I have only done what I absolutely had to do, mostly for appearances. Nothing in this world is going to stand in my way to protect the things that I love. I did shoot dad, but I had to, the Chinese merc's were gonna kill him. I had no control over those wackos. It was all Colonel Tapper. He and Zeus had the whole thing planned out. Tapper hired the Chinese when his SEAL team failed to bring any artifacts out of the aurora. He used money diverted from dad's accounts to pay for it all. Whether you believe me or not, the fact is, Colonel Tapper is going to cripple the United States military. Valhalla is capable of that and so much more. If the U.S. goes up against Valhalla and loses, and it will lose, enemies from around the world will come out of hiding to feed on its bloated carcass. I have tried to send out warnings through the councillors here, but when I asked them for help, they didn't believe me. They thought I had ulterior motives. Valhalla is in Tapper's control, Odin's thirst for new warriors has been wetted and now he is running around the world just looking to pick a fight."

"Look, Indy, brother... we can change all of that. Dad is safe now, and so is your mom. We are indestructible and we have limitless power and money at our fingertips. We can do whatever we want, take revenge on Tapper, topple Valhalla... we could even rule the world. Together we are unbeatable, what do you say, will you stand with me, brother?"

Chapter 16 – Eden - Amber Awakening

Doc sat beside his son who lay on the bed unmoving and unresponsive. Warren was pale as a ghost, but all his vital signs showed he was alive and well. It was as if he was sleeping and unable to wake. Doc sat down after checking his son's vital signs for the twentieth time and put his head in his hands.

"I don't understand, it should have worked by now," he said to the air.

Warren had been sleeping for over twelve hours now and nothing Doc had been able to do could wake him. Doc hadn't left his side since the crystal shell had melted away. Occasionally Warren would mutter in his sleep or toss and turn but what had really worried Doc was the moans. Several times Warren had begun to moan, it was a low guttural moan that raised the hair on Doc's arms. The moaning would last for minutes until Warren stopped moving again and slept.

Someone on the other side of the curtains cleared their throat to announce their presence.

"Doc, it's me Cindy. Is there anything I can get you?"

Cindy was one of the volunteer nurses that had made it out of the castle. Her red head poked through the curtains and she flashed Doc a brilliant smile.

"You haven't eaten all day, you need to keep your energy up so I brought you a little snack. Hank left some of his pie and cider next door and there is just enough left for you."

She smiled again and stepped into the room to hand Doc a tray.

"No change eh?" Cindy asked as she looked down on Warren.

"No," Doc said as he dug into the pie.

In between mouthfuls he said, "Nothing's changed... although he looks like he might be coming around at any time now. His body temperature has gone up several degrees and his pulse is quickening. With any luck he will be up soon."

Doc's voice wasn't very convincing and he dropped his eyes when Cindy looked his way.

"Hey, if you need a break, I can watch over him for a bit." Cindy offered.

"Thank you Cindy, but I am not leaving his side until he wakes."

Doc nodded once, making it final, no arguments.

Cindy didn't argue, but instead left the room in search of a chair. She pulled it up on the opposite side of the bed with a defiant look on her face.

"If you change your mind, I am here," she reminded him.

Doc could only smile back at the devious woman. She had always been helpful and so out going. Being around her was easy, there was no pressure like with his other colleagues. Cindy was a great listener, but she really knew how to carry a conversation. That was one of Doc's failings, he always felt awkward in most conversations. The best part about this woman was she knew when he needed silence. They could sit in a room together and not speak, and he felt no need to entertain her. If only his ex-wife had been more like Cindy, what a mistake that one had been. His ex-wife Laura had been a great catch at the time. She was young, beautiful and working as an intern when they had first met. Laura was perfect for him, until she left him for another man. She had abandoned him and left him to raise Warren as a single overworked father. Warren had grown up without a mom in his life and a father that had to work long hours because of his job.

Doc's thoughts were interrupted by another low moan from Warren. The moaning seemed to get louder this time until Warren began thrashing around uncontrollably in his bed. Both Doc and Cindy jumped from their chairs to hold Warren still so he would not fall off the bed and hurt himself.

Cindy fell back from the bed with a little shriek. Doc looked up from Warren to see what was wrong. Cindy was pointing at Warren's face, at his mouth.

"Look at his teeth!" She yelled.

Doc looked down at his son and had to lift Warren's lip to get a better view of his teeth. Doc sucked in a breath when he saw that Warren's teeth had crystalized. It wasn't the normal clear white crystal though, this was a dark amber color, with just a tinge of red.

"What in god's name?" Doc cursed.

Warren's eyes popped open as his teeth snapped down, narrowly missing Doc's finger. Doc fell back into the blanket curtains in shock as he looked into Warren's eyes. Even his eyes had taken on the strange crystal coating.

The sight chilled Doc to the bone and the moaning only made it worse. Struggling to free himself from the blankets, Doc was slow to react. Warren slowly sat up right and looked around the room with his odd eyes. When the amber eyes settled on Cindy, a wicked smile curled his lips.

"Cindy," he said. "I need help... I can't breathe."

Warren held his chest with both hands as Cindy rushed to his side. Warren began to cough uncontrollably, bloody spittle forming on his lips. Cindy supported him and rubbed his back as the coughing lessened.

"Thank you... Cindy... that's better." Warren said as he lay back down. "My throat is on fire, can... I get something to drink..."

Cindy reached for Doc's glass of Cider and lifted it to Warren's lips. Warren took several long gulps and then released a long sigh.

"Thank you." He turned to see his dad, stumbling out of the curtains. "Dad? What's wrong? Are you okay? You're white as a ghost."

Doc continued to stare at his son. With great effort, he calmed his nerves and closed his gaping mouth. Doc forced himself to walk to his son's side but refrained from actually making contact with the boy.

"Warren, how do you feel? Tell me everything, go on."

Warren nodded once and said, "I feel a bit weird, kind of fuzzy I guess you could say. I have this weird taste in my mouth and I am having a real hard time breathing. It's like a bad chest cold. Everything looks weird too. Where are we anyway and what is with the wacky orange lights?"

Warren looked around the room at several light sources before turning to his father, waiting for an explanation.

Doc didn't know what to say so he avoided the question and turned to Cindy.

"Cindy would you be a dear and go get Dr. Howard from upstairs. Make sure you tell him to bring his bag. The whole bag."

Cindy left the room in a rush. Doc turned back to his son and put a hand on his forehead.

"Son, I think you might have a bit of an infection. We are going to give you some medicine to clear it up, so don't worry. You'll be fine."

"But I feel fine dad, I feel like I could lift a house. I'm really starving though, just tell me how to get to the fridge and I will go grab something real quick."

Doc put a hand on his son's chest to stop him from rising.

"Warren, you stay put, that's an order. We don't need you getting sick again just when I got you back. You stay put, and that's final."

Warren nodded silently and relaxed back into the bed.

"I do feel kinda off," he said. "Almost like I am moving in slow motion." Warren raised a hand and moved it slowly around the air in front of his face.

"It's so weird, I am trying to move fast, but I just can't." Warren looked up at his dad. "Did you drug me or something? This is pretty freaky."

"No son," Doc said. "No drugs yet. I have to run a couple of tests, but Dr. Howard is bringing a couple things down to help. Just sit still. Close your eyes and try to relax."

Warren did as he was told and slid back into a restless sleep within seconds. Doc looked down at his son and wondered how bad the infection was. Even Warren's fingernails had begun to turn a ruddy orange color.

"Damn it where is that Howard?" Doc cursed as he sat down to wait.

Chapter 17 – Eden / Valhalla - We Have to Go Back.

Indy and James stood face to face on the castle roof, neither one moving or saying anything. Indy considered James offer. He could see how James had been given a rough life, and how events had spiralled out of control. If Indy rejected him now, James would have nowhere left to turn. He knew James had a bad streak, but now... he was family.

"Fine," Indy said. "We will work together for now but there are conditions, first thing first, we have to free dad.

James shook his head.

"No, dad's statue is locked up in his safe room until this mess is sorted. I need to clear my name if I ever have a hope of earning his respect. Anyway he is safer there for the time being."

Indy considered his words and nodded his head in agreement.

"Okay then what is the first step. What is your plan, brother?"

"Colonel Tapper is packing up shop, he has recalled all his teams back to Valhalla, except for mine. As Guardian of Valhalla I have certain duties..."

Indy interrupted with a laugh.

"I forgot you are a Guardian. Did anyone tell you I was Eden's Guardian...? I mean what are the chances that the two of us..."

James smacked Indy on the shoulder, hard enough to make him sway on his feet.

"Stop interrupting, you're as bad as your mom." James smiled at his brother, easing the tension. "Okay here is the plan, we need to take Colonel Tapper out of the picture. He is the one behind everything, we take him out and then get Odin to make Valhalla disappear. The world goes back to normal and we can pull dad out of hibernation."

Indy thought about the plan, it sounded good but there were several loose ends.

"I need to find Joslyn first, she was trapped in the tunnels after I stole some of that golden ale."

James looked sideways at his little brother.

"She your girlfriend now?"

"Kinda," Indy replied. "It's complicated right now, but I need to make sure she is ok."

James shook his head and placed a hand on Indy's shoulder.

"We searched the tunnels after your little escapade down there. I knew exactly which way you got out of the castle, I designed the underground tunnels after all. There was no sign of anyone down there... nothing, no bodies, nothing. I am sorry."

James released his grip as Indy's shoulders slumped.

"I need to find her James, I can't leave here until I do."

"We don't have time for that right now. Our rides are almost here."

Indy was about to disagree but James stopped him.

"I will send the Valkyries back to search for her, I swear we will find her."

Indy nodded numbly, still unsure if he could really trust his brother but deciding for now, he really had no choice. He needed to deal with Valhalla first.

James checked the sky once before turning back to regard Indy.

"You know, the one thing that bothers me is why did you break into the castle just to steal that little bit of ale? I mean the stuff really isn't that good. Not like those apples, Adam gave me. This stuff only gives you a couple days of freedom outside of the aurora."

"Naw, it wasn't for us," Indy said with a smirk. "Doc wanted it to get Warren out of the crystal statue, once he gave it to him the crystal stuff just melted away."

"Ahh that makes more sense. So I take it that is why you were up here, you came to rescue dad."

Indy nodded his head and produced a flask filled with the golden liquid.

"A smear across the lips and then a bit in the mouth does the trick. We saw you do it to Warren's eye."

James shook his head, "Clever, very clever." James checked his watch. "The Valkyries are due back any second. Don't make eye contact with the ones in black, they are a bit... chippy."

At the word Valkyrie, Indy remembered Jon. He turned from James and rushed to the spot Jon had been speared. His body was gone. Indy looked around but he found nothing, there wasn't even a spot of blood to be found.

James came up behind him.

"Jon will be okay, I saw one of the white Valkyries with him during the fight. She has already taken him to Valhalla. Those silver spears are tricky little things. Odin himself commands them and selects their targets. I don't know why he targeted your friend but I doubt Jon will remember us the next time we see him. James looked up into the sky and pointed at a pair of large winged creatures descending. The Valkyries black feathered wings beat the air as they landed on the castle's roof.

James nodded to each Valkyrie in turn before introducing them to Indy.

"Indy I want you to meet two of my very good friends-

"Hello again Freya, Lana," Indy said and gave them both his best lopsided grin after interrupting his brother again.

If the Valkyries were surprised to see Indy alive, they gave no clue.

Instead Freyja turned to James and said, "Odin demands your presence in the throne room, Guardian. Prepare yourselves for transit."

Lana said nothing but gave Indy a little wink. Then the two Valkyries reached for the brothers and lifted them into the air. A wall of emotion tightened Indy's stomach as he was lifted into the air. As the ground receded below his vision began to swim and waver. Black spots appeared behind his eyes and anxiety started his body shaking.

James called to him, "Still having trouble with that little phobia of yours? Take a sip from that flask of yours, it will strengthen your will."

Indy did as James suggested and uncapped the little flask. As he tipped it to his lips, the flask in his hand rattled slightly. Puzzled at the noise, Indy peered into its depths and noticed an odd amber crystal coating the lip of the flask. He was about to dump some of the bottle's contents into his hand when he lost his grip on the flask and it tumbled away to the ground. Indy looked up from the falling flask as the fear of heights returned. It was all he could do just to squeeze his eyes closed and pretend he was in a better place.

James called out to his brother as the Valkyries bore them higher, bringing Indy out of his trance.

"Indy, find the warmth of your dragon in your mind. Have it? Good, now ask him to appear in your palm and stay there. Once we leave the aurora, your dragon is going to re-crystalize out of your skin. Try not to drop it before we pass back into Valhalla's aurora, okay?"

Indy nodded and looked down into his palm. It was better to focus on something other than the ground far below. He called to the dragon with his mind and watched as its black form swirled out onto his open palm. The dragon

curled up in the middle of his palm and waited.
Its red eyes gleaming as it stared back at Indy.

Chapter 18 – Valhalla - Guardian Sticks

James and Indy were escorted into Odin's throne room, a massive room at the very top of the tower section of the fortress. The room was open to the skies and thick marble columns held a golden dome above. As Indy looked up into the rafters of the dome, he could see various large birds roosting in the shadows. Around the room were several large braziers burning with massive golden flames.

Ahead of him sitting on the throne at the center of the room was Odin. Standing beside Odin was Kara and kneeling before the throne was Colonel Tapper and Tsu. Tapper was wearing a dark blue navel uniform that had his rank and various medals pinned onto the chest. Tsu was wearing a strange black cloak that had thick silver veins running in seemingly random patterns throughout the dark material. He also had his samurai sword strapped across his back. Kara was the first to see Indy and the joy that spread across her face warmed Indy's heart.

Odin waved the black Valkyries forth when he spotted them entering the throne room.

"Freyja my dear, you have kept us waiting, but thank you for fetching my wayward Guardian. James you have been away too long, kneel before the throne and let us have your report."

Odin's one good eye moved from James to Indy and a hard scowl crossed Odin's face.

"Little hero? I thought I had you dropped into the sea."

Odin turned to look at Kara with a suspicious glance. Odin turned back and looked a little closer at Indy, leaning forward in his massive throne.

"My, my, my... aren't you full of surprises... Guardian." Odin said and then leaned back in his chair. "I was wondering why Adam had not sent forth his champion."

Odin smiled at Indy and said, "Well, I supposed Little Hero won't suit for an emissary of Eden now would it?"

Indy shook his head.

"My name is Daniel Locke."

The name had a ring of truth to it now that his father was in hibernation and out of the picture. He supposed that for the time being he would leave the Junior part off the end of his name.

"Daniel Locke, I officially welcome you as a guest of Valhalla." Odin said with a small bow. "We will have a feast in your honour-

Daniel cut the master of Valhalla off in mid-sentence. "Forgive me Odin, but we have pressing matters to attend to first."

Odin glared at the interruption but he waved Indy to continue.

"I am not sure what your agents have been telling you, but what you are doing here is wrong." Indy began, he watched Odin turn a nasty red color but hold his tongue. "I have been told a bit about what Valhalla is all about and from my understanding, basically you are training an army that will defend Earth in its darkest hour. Part of Valhalla's design is to help safeguard the human race from extinction, correct?"

Odin nodded once and waited for Indy to continue.

"What you fail to realise is that, as of this moment, Valhalla is only contributing to the problems. I don't mean to tell you your business, but if you were to remove Valhalla from the picture, I might be able to get the armies of the world to stand down."

Colonel Tapper rose from his spot along with Tsu as Indy talked. Tapper had quite enough of listening to Indy though.

"We need the absolute best warriors to fight in Ragnarok. The only way we can find these warriors is through open combat. The world is on the brink of nuclear war, the entire human population could be eradicated in a heartbeat. Where would you get your warriors then Odin? I have seen your army and I must say I am not impressed."

"Silence grey man or I will have your tongue." Odin said as his temper flared.

Odin turned from Tapper to look pointedly at Indy.

"The old man is insubordinate but he has a point Guardian. Without warriors, Valhalla is nothing. We must continue to select heroes to fill out ranks before it is too late."

"I have a suggestion," Indy said darting a quick look at his brother. "What if we were to hold a tournament, like the trials, but instead of killing the losers, we use the tournament to fill the Halls of the Heroes. If Valhalla were to say... disappear for a bit, I am sure tensions would ease. If I am wrong, well, I suppose you could just reappear and start collecting again. Just give it a chance Odin. I will do everything in my power to make it work. You have my word."

"The word of a child and the word of a loser." Colonel Tapper mocked. "I thought Valhalla was a mountain of strength, not a pile of trash."

Odin stood up from his throne and flexed his muscled arms. A brilliant spear of silver flashed into existence in his hands.

"You dare insult Valhalla!" he yelled.

Odin reared back his arm to throw as Colonel Tapper dropped to the floor and begged for forgiveness.

"Please Odin, hear me out. I wish only to..."

"You want a show of power," Odin said. "Then you must prove to me who has the stronger argument. As is fitting humans always have the choice, no matter what happens, that fact will always remain true. We have two conflicting views however, and since we are in Valhalla, you will settle the matter as is fitting. Select your champion and battle to the death. The winner shall decide how Valhalla acts in the future. Guardian of Eden, do you chose to champion your own cause or will you choose an avatar to fight in your place?" Odin asked.

"I will stand for Eden's Guardian." James said as he stepped up beside his brother.

Indy nodded at his brother and said, "Thank you James, but this is my fight. I would be grateful to have you at my side though."

"Done," Odin said. "And what of you Colonel? Will you battle this... child, this loser yourself?"

Colonel Tapper took one look at Indy and shrugged.

"I am passed my fighting years Odin, I will choose another to take my place."

Tapper looked at the man at his side and said, "Tsu will fight for my honour."

"Done." Odin said with a loud booming voice. "Valkyries, prepare the floor, there is no time like the present to settle this matter."

Odin raised his voice even further and bellowed, "Gammon! Gammon! Bring me the Guardian sticks."

Gammon appeared from the entrance behind them with a large leather wrapped bundle. Bowing he placed the bundle at Odin's feet. Gammon rose and as he was backing from the room, caught Indy's eye. Gammon's face didn't betray an ounce of surprise at Indy's appearance but as he left the room, Gammon gave Indy a wide smile.

"Since some people are notoriously hard to kill..." Odin said as he kicked open the leather bundle.

Inside lay four golden sticks, two had black raven's feathers and the other two had white swan feathers.

"These weapons will deplete your physical energy every time you take a hit. The winner will be decided by knockout. The loser will be cast out of Valhalla, and into the sea... in an area WITHOUT an aurora." Odin looked meaningfully at Kara. "Valkyries choose your champion."

Kara and Freyja stepped to the golden sticks and picked up their respective color. With a nod, they turned and walked to their champions. Indy's heart did a little dance when Kara started his way. The white feathers attached to the fighting sticks danced in the breeze as she walked.

"Your weapons, Guardian." Kara said as she bowed low and offered the weapons.

"Thank you Valkyrie." Indy said and flashed her his lopsided grin along with a wink. He was not disappointed when her smile brightened and she winked back.

"Guardians ready?" Odin called.

Indy and Tsu had their weapons held high and nodded at Odin.

"Begin!"

Indy tapped his two sticks together, expecting a sudden burst of electricity. Nothing happened. Across from him, Tsu started forward, his sticks whirling.

"Not like the dragon sticks I guess," Indy thought to himself moments before Tsu struck.

The golden fighting sticks were heavy and thick but incredibly easy to swing. When the sticks stuck each other, they rang with a sharp crack, almost like mini bursts of thunder. Tsu lunged forward and tried to bury both ends of the sticks in Indy's belly. Indy just barely moved out of range in time. Stretching out and swinging Indy found he had a slight reach advantage as he clipped Tsu in the shoulder. Tsu sprung away from the blow and looked at Indy, his eyes full of menace. The fight continued in a whirlwind, neither fighter landing any solid blows but each taking several glancing shots. Indy could feel his arms weakening from the effort. Even his breathing began to suffer as Indy fought to control his heaving chest.

Indy looked at Tsu and tried to determine if the other Guardian was having any of the same issues. However, Tsu's face was a mask of concentration and his breathing was calm and quiet.

Indy was going to have to make a move soon, or risk running out of strength. He had an idea, but it would be a win or lose move. Indy backed off a bit from the fight and as Tsu came toward him, only defended himself. He continued backtracking while Tsu leapt after the advantage. Tsu must have sensed Indy's weakness and was eager to finish the fight. Indy was waiting for the right moment and when it came, he was ready. Tsu attempted his two handed stomach shot again and this time, Indy let the ends of the sticks connect. The blow didn't hit hard but it was enough to drive the air from his lungs.

Indy dropped his left stick to the ground and grabbed at Tsu's sticks buried in his gut. As he grabbed the sticks, Indy swivelled and brought his remaining fighting stick down on Tsu's wrists with the last bit of strength he had in him. When they connected with Tsu's wrists, the room filled with a thunderclap that shook the floor.

Tsu's mouth fell open and his sticks fell from his limp hands. Indy took advantage of the shock and stepped into a backhanded swing that would have been a homerun in any park. Tsu took the golden stick right in the face and slid backward across the floor.

Tsu shook his head trying to clear his vision and reached under his cloak. He pulled out a thin metal grenade and popped the pin. Tsu threw the flash bang in front of Indy. As the grenade went off Indy watched Tsu rise from the ground and pull the samurai sword free from its sheath.

That's when the battle changed. Indy raised his sticks as the flash bang went off and he began to charge through the smoky cloud towards Tsu unhindered by the flash of light or the concussive blast. When Indy got to the other side of the smoke, Tsu was gone.

The samurai sword came out of nowhere. It struck Indy three times in one heartbeat. It rang off his head, his shoulder and then his arm. Luckily, the sword did no damage to him. Indy spun away from the blows and swung one of the sticks at where Tsu should have been. He was not there, he wasn't anywhere Indy could see. A blur moved at him from behind one of the golden fires. Indy wasn't sure what it was, it was moving so fast. A flash of black and silver and then he was hit by the sword three more times. As the blur broke away again, Indy followed. Indy watched in amazement as the blur stopped moving for a moment near the fire. Tsu stood motionless regarding Indy with a slight smile on his face. The samurai sword reflected the fires golden light as Tsu held it aloft.

"Nice trick, but you aren't gonna win like that Tsu." Indy said and waved the warrior forward.

Tsu stopped to consider Indy's words. "You are right, things have changed since our last fight... Guardian."

Tsu eyed the sticks in Indy's hand and let his glance slide across the floor to where his own matching sticks were laying.

They both moved towards the fallen sticks at the same time, but Tsu moved with eye blurring speed and was there much faster. Indy pulled up short to see Tsu holding the sword in one hand and a golden stick in the other.

Then he attacked. The stick moved fast, really fast and smacked into Indy three times, the last strike aimed at his wrists. The white feathered dragon sticks clattered to the floor as Indy felt his strength rush out of him and the room grew dark. Indy dropped to one knee and he sensed Tsu standing over him, but there was nothing he could do.

Indy raised his head and in a moment of clarity saw Kara watching him. Kara was not weeping, or even worried, she was strong. Kara was proud and Indy knew right then and there, he was still her champion. Since the moment he stepped into Valhalla, the bond they shared had been muted. Nevertheless, it was still there. Even face to face, he could only detect a small trace of her emotions, just enough to let him know that they were still somehow connected. In the instant his body hit the floor the bond flared again. It was as if a dam had burst and all the pent up emotions flooded in. Anger, pain, pride, sadness and sorrow washed over him and gave him strength. But what lifted his body off the floor was her love. It shone like the sun and burned through him like a fire. There was nothing he could imagine that could ever compare to that one surge of power he felt then and there. Certainly there was no one living that could stand before him now.

Tsu was looking to Odin with a wide smile on his face, waiting for the one eyed warrior to declare him the victor. Odin simply stared right through Tsu with his blue eye and gave an almost imperceptible shake of his head. Frustrated Tsu raised the black feathered Guardian stick over his head and brought it down on Indy.

Indy reached out and grabbed the stick in mid swing. With a tug, he pulled Tsu down on top of him, using Tsu's incredible momentum against him. Indy rolled with the smaller man and kicked out as they landed. Tsu went flying into one of the fiery braziers, knocking it over in the process. Both the sword and the stick flew off in different directions as Tsu tried to bat the fires off his black cloak.

Indy rose from the ground and charged at Tsu, not looking for a weapon but instead putting his entire focus on Tsu and nothing else. He ran through the liquid fire that had spilled from the brazier and chased down Tsu. The liquid clung to his legs and spread up his body to engulf him as he ran. He was a human torch, a fireball that was homing in on his target. Indy's first punch landed on Tsu's chin with a thud and was followed by another strike to his chest. The fire splattered off him with every hit, splashing the ground and creating little mini fires around them. Indy didn't stop throwing punches but neither did Tsu sit by and take the punishment. The fight turned into a brawl. Kicks and punches landed or were deflected. Tsu tried grappling with the fire soaked Indy but had to release his hold as his hands started to burn.

Tsu landed a large windmill kick that turned Indy away for the briefest moment before he was back on him again. The fallen sword must have given Tsu the supernatural speed because without it when he turned to run, Indy was only steps behind. Indy slid forward to scissor kick Tsu's legs and brought the running man down hard.

Indy's vision started to go red as a new emotion crept over him, anger. The rage boiled in his mind as he stalked Tsu. Kicking him, punching him, and throwing him around the room. The fires around Indy burned themselves out as the two warriors fought their way to the center of the room.

Tsu was beaten and they all knew it. But that was when Tsu played his last trick. The black cloak swirled as he performed a backflip away from Indy and then the cloak itself came free and fluttered to the ground leaving Indy to look around the room for his missing opponent.

A sharp intake of breath told Indy where to look though. Tsu had pulled a knife from his belt and was holding it against Kara's throat. There was only the muted sense of anger coming through the bond. Whatever had caused the rush of emotions before was gone again.

"Not another step Locke or the bird gets carved." Tsu said with a sneer.

Indy did as he was told. However, Odin was a totally different matter. The massive warrior was beside himself with rage.

"You dare assault one of my Valkyries!" He yelled as a silver spear materialized in his hand.

"Quiet you blustering Cyclops. You will sit back in that chair and shut your mouth. Or do you forget who you have named Guardian?"

"You forget you are not the only Guardian here Tsu." James said as he stepped forward, the black helmet on his head again, radiating shadows around the room.

Tsu nodded once but kept the blade tight to Kara's throat.

"So we have a stalemate. Fine, I will withdraw from Valhalla for the time being." Tsu snaked his free hand down to Kara's waist and retrieved the flask inlaid with golden leaves. I will take this ale and my hostage with me. Don't try to follow or I will kill her."

Tsu guided Kara to the edge of the tower and wrapped his free arm around her waist. The room was motionless as Tsu waited for Kara to spread her wings and fly them away. No one else moved or even breathed. Indy watched the pair carefully, looking, waiting... needing an opening.

It was Kara that ignited the next flurry of motion. She smiled sadly at Indy and then winked one beautiful brown eye at him. When she raised her hand to wave goodbye Indy noticed a little metal ring around her index finger.

A second later, the grenade went off. The force of the blast threw Kara to the side and Tsu back towards the lip of the tower. The blast had forced Tsu to his knees but the man was quick to recover. He already had one hand coming up with a small black gun in it. He was looking towards Kara and lifting the gun when Indy crashed into him.

Together they toppled off the tower and plummeted to the rooftops below. They fell from the highest section of the tower and tumbled through the air over one hundred feet. The force of the landing cracked the stone rooftop around them and raised a thick cloud of dust.

The Valkyries descended from the tower and lifted the two limp Guardians back to the upper platform. Freyja cradled Indy's motionless body and placed him at the foot of Odin's throne. Lana dropped Tsu's broken form at the center of the ring, waiting for further orders.

James rushed forward to Indy's side and fell to his knees.

"You did it Indy! That was amazing! Indy?"

Indy opened one eye and looked around the room. He looked back to his brother and asked, "Kara?"

James shook his head, "She was cut pretty bad, and they were taking her to the pond to heal her. Odin said she is going to live, but he wasn't sure if she would make it to the ponds in time."

"In time for what?" Indy asked confused. "You said she was going to live."

"Yes, she will live, but if they don't make it to the ponds in time they will have to give her the potion of rebirth. Indy... the potion will heal her, but it will also erase her memory... she won't remember you... she won't remember any of this. Valkyries don't wear memory charms."

Indy stared in disbelief at James. He looked from his brother to Odin, who nodded in confirmation.

Odin stepped from his throne and reached down to pluck Indy off the ground with one massive hand. The warmth of Odin's hand leaked into Indy's body and he was instantly reenergized. Odin set him down on his feet and patted his shoulder.

"We have a lot to discuss Guardian. Come down to my chambers and we will await news from the Valkyries. There are several other things we need to discuss in the meanwhile."

Odin turned to the remaining Valkyries and waved them to Tsu's body.

"To the skies, let heaven hold out its hand and cradle the lost. May its light forever shine in memory of the fallen."

The Valkyries bore Tsu from the room and out into the skies.

"Hang on, where did Tapper go?" James asked as he looked around the room.

The old military man had disappeared and was nowhere to be found.

Indy looked around at the room and noticed one other thing was missing as well.

"Looks like he grabbed that samurai sword too."

Odin narrowed his eyes in concentration and then sighed loudly. "The grey man has left Valhalla. I cannot sense him anywhere on the island."

Chapter 19 – Wish No Wish

Doc woke with a start, and for a second, he could not remember where he was. He looked around at the empty room and when he noticed the empty bed, he shot to his feet. He was on the third level of the tower. He must have dozed off while waiting for his son Warren to wake again. Now his son was gone.

"Warren? Warren where are you?" Doc called out.

Silence. Nothing made a sound or even moved that he could hear. It was odd to hear the tower like that. Normally there was at least some activity, someone coming or going. The silence was eerie.

Doc stood tall and stretched, his muscles ached from the way he had slept.

"How long was I asleep?" He muttered into the gloomy room.

A noise thudded once somewhere on the level above. Well at least someone was around, maybe they could tell him where Warren had gone. Doc remembered Dr. Howard had been examining his son just before he had dozed off. Maybe they had been able to wake his son and gotten him up and out of bed for some exercise. Of course, they would have left me to sleep, Cindy had probably insisted on it. That sweet, sweet woman. Doc grinned in anticipation of his son's recovery and wandered up the stairs to the upper level.

As soon as he set foot onto the next level, Doc knew something was wrong. Equipment had been scattered across the floor, and the tables were over turned. Still there was no one in sight. Doc heard a small shuffling coming from the far side of the room. Unsure what it was, he edged closer. As he rounded the large table, he saw a small black dog. He recognized the little mutt instantly. It was one of the animals from the hydro plant's experiment labs. Back when a Navy SEAL team ransacked his lab, all those animals had been released into the wild. But what the heck was it doing here?

The dog's head came up suddenly as Doc stepped on a piece of crumpled paper. Doc's breath caught in his throat as the dog's eyes landed on him, the dog's orange eyes. Looking at those eyes chilled him to the bone and raised the hair on the back of his neck. On a man, the eyes are a window to the soul. A thousand words can be said in a glance. On this thing, this dog, only one word came to mind... doom.

The dog came tearing across the floor at him and Doc's chest began to pound. He was frozen in fear and couldn't even think to begin to run. Doc uttered a cry as something brushed past his leg from behind. It was his little Minotaur, Torn. Torn raced by on its hooved feet and intercepted the black dog with a loud smack. The little Minotaur ran over the bigger dog and casually tossed the dog across the room. Torn came racing back to stand protectively in front of Doc's legs as the black dog got slowly back to its feet.

Clearly over matched the little dog put its tail between its legs and ran off up the stairs.

Doc looked down at his little protector and smiled.

"Thank you Torn."

The Minotaur huffed and then sprinted up the side of an over turned table and leapt back towards Doc. It caught hold of the long lab coat and pulled itself into one of Doc's large pockets, disappearing from sight. Doc smiled again and patted the bulging pocket before heading up the stairs in search of his son.

The upper level of the tower was empty, save for a little white box and a little man in a three-piece suit.

"Adam?" Doc asked, not believing his eyes.

"Yes Henrik, it's me." Adam looked as if he were about to cry but offered him a slight smile. "I am afraid I am the bearer of bad news."

Doc took a deep breath before asking, "Tell me, is it my son? Is he dead?"

Adam shook his head. "No, your son is still alive. The bad news is that he is infected with a very deadly disease. Warren will not die from the disease, he is... a carrier."

Doc let his breath out in one long sigh. "That's good, his death would have been the end of me." Doc confessed. "When Warren's mother left me I..."

Adam held out a hand to forestall Doc's rambling.

"Your son is capable of bringing life on this planet to an end." Adams voice rang out in a loud singsong that echoed off the walls.

Doc just stared at the little curly haired boy as if he was mad.

"If Warren leaves Eden, he will begin a chain reaction of events that among other things, could lead to the eradication of humans worldwide."

"This disease is that bad?" Doc asked not daring to breathe again.

Adam nodded his head in agreement.

"Is there anything we can do?"

Adams face brightened slightly and he nodded. "I am not permitted to act directly, but I can offer you a choice. I want to warn you that I do not condone killing, but I can suggest a few options."

Adam walked over to touch the white box in the center of the room.

"This box can make anything you wish. For example, it could cure your son, or it could create a weapon that would strike him dead. If you choose to save him, you risk letting him leave the aurora. There are many other things you could wish for, the box can make almost anything you could dream of. There are several things it cannot do and many more things that we don't have time for. You only get one wish. Do not wish for more than one thing, the results can be disastrous."

"Where is he right now? Is he safe?" Doc begged.

"Warren is currently blasting his way through the briar wall. The disease has affected his mind but not his intelligence. The young man has expropriated several weapons and artifacts that had been stored here in this very tower. I don't know why he is so desperate to leave Eden but he will be outside the aurora's influence in mere moments. You must choose quickly."

Doc rubbed his face with his hand and stared at the ceiling. Then he took a long look at Adam and the white box.

Adam seemed to read his mind and said, "I cannot seal Eden's borders, nor can I force Warren to turn back. You must accomplish this task on your own. I can only provide you with the tools with which to work."

Doc knew he had to choose between killing or saving Warren, Adam had made that fairly obvious. He tried to let his mind think it through, there had to be another way, he just had to think.

"You only have seconds before he is through the aurora Henrik."

Doc knew what he had to wish for, he knew it in his heart. Warren needed to die before he could spread the disease. But he couldn't do it, he just couldn't. With a shudder, Doc's mind and body failed him and he crashed to the floor in a sobbing heap.

Doc lay there crying, refusing to look at Adam or the box. Refusing to look upon the world he had failed.

A soft hand caressed his cheek and then lifted his chin so that he was looking into Adam's eyes.

"Be at peace Henrik. All is not lost. There are always other choices, other wishes." Adam pulled a golden apple from inside his suit jacket and slid it into Doc's hand. "This will allow you to follow your son. Take a small bite every couple of days and you will not crystalize. Once you find your son, feed him whatever remains of the apple, including the core. It will prevent the disease from spreading any further."

Adam patted Doc's grey hair as he curled his old wrinkled hands around the golden apple.

"Do not tarry, the disease spreads as we speak." Adam said in a soft whisper.

When Doc raised his head to say he would hurry, but Adam was already gone. So too, was the white box.

Doc stared at the golden apple resting in his hands. It was the only hope he had left for his son.

Chapter 20 – Valhalla - Odin's Message

Odin's private chambers were not unlike the other rooms in Valhalla, with a few notable exceptions. The room was large, and the furniture had been built for a man of Odin's stature. A long wooden table dominated the center of the room. James and Indy strode the length of the room to where Odin stood warming himself in front of a massive fireplace. He turned when they paused a few feet from his back.

"Welcome Guardians," he said in a grave tone. "I will not be hearing your proposal concerning trials and tournaments. As of right now Valhalla's borders are closed."

Indy and James looked at one another and then back to Odin. They crossed their arms at the same time and waited for more information.

Odin looked over the Guardians one by one and then nodded his head.

"I see that Adam has made a wise choice in selecting you Daniel. I can sense much power in you and your brother. There is a darkness in you that will have to be controlled, but a warrior's spirit is never a gentle one. A word of warning though, things are going to get much worse before they get better."

Odin waved his two massive hands and the wall behind him vanished, fireplace and all. It was replaced by a gigantic picture window. Outside the window, it showed several different scenes in each of the windows panes. In every scene, there was chaos. Flooding in city streets, volcanoes spewing ash into the sky, buildings toppled by massive earthquakes.

"You have not felt the earth shudder, because you are on a floating island. Those on the ground have felt the earth heaving under their feet for several hours now."

Odin pointed at one of the panels and the view switched to a large familiar mountain in Japan. Half of Mount Fuji was gone, and smoke was pouring from a massive crater.

Indy and James stood in stunned silence as the images rolled across the window. It was a global disaster, like none they had ever seen.

"What... What happened?" Indy asked. "What caused all this?"

A flash of light from behind them lit the window for a moment and a soft singsong voice answered Indy's question.

"The Hades tower has activated. The tower was sealed away at the heart of the mountain known as Fuji. Hades is not like Eden or even similar to Valhalla. Hades itself is tied to the earth's mantle. As we speak, it is expanding its reach through the earth's crust, creating a spider web of tunnels under every populated community on earth."

"Why, what is its purpose?" Indy asked. "I thought each tower was supposed to safe guard the people of earth. All I see here is destruction and chaos."

"Most of the damage you see here is superficial. Although many structures and properties will be damaged, casualties and actual deaths will be no different than any other day on this world. The Hades tower is setting up a network in order to contain a population critical event. An infection so bad that if left uncontained, will eventually wipe out life on this planet as you know it."

"It will be the duty of the Guardians to contain outbreaks and then activate a network tendril to cleanse the area. We will have to find other methods of containing the infection, as of now there is only one way." Odin said pointing at the black helmet under James's arm. "Some artifacts are capable of a temporary field generation. Aurora's like that can be used to limit infections, once inside an aurora, the infection will not be allowed to leave due to the crystallization process."

"Now for the bad news," Adam said as his smiled disappeared. "I know the source of the infection and the manner in which it spreads. I will work with Odin to see if we can come up with a possible cure. I warn you right now it is more than likely that anyone infected and claimed by Hades will not see the light of day again."

"The source..." Indy gently reminded Adam.

"Warren Hocking has consumed a rather odd cocktail and has been subjected to a hibernation orb. The combination of these things along with an infection in his nasal cavity has led to a unique and devastating ailment."

"The golden ale running through his blood has been contaminated by a self-regenerating amber crystal, the crystal has spread through his red blood cells and has mutated to become the infection. The ale also acts as a temporary crystallization inhibitor."

Odin growled softly deep in his chest and Adam patted the large man's forearm.

"The ale has allowed him to leave the confines of Eden's aurora without crystalizing. Warren, along with his father Doctor Hocking and several others have taken the concoction or have been infected by Warren. Due to the aurora, Eden will contain most of the infected, preventing them from migrating through the area and infecting more of earth's population. Of those infected, only the people who have drunk the tainted golden ale will escape to spread the disease."

"Which way are they heading?" Indy asked as a feeling of dread spread slowly over him.

"I am not certain but if they remain on the same course they were last seen on... Appleton."

THE END

Acknowledgments

Larry, Dianne, Trish, Rylie, Keira, Lindsey, Kevin, Tanner, Serge, Scott, Jen, Jennrz, Casey, Matt, Gary, Luc, Erin, Tina and Keith.

BIOGRAPHY

"Indy" author Marty Longson is the author of the Daniel Locke Science Fiction / Fantasy series. Marty graduated from the University of Windsor and St. Clair College. He lives in Windsor, Ontario with his wife and two young daughters.

WWW.MARTYLONGSON.COM

Made in the USA
Charleston, SC
16 June 2014